She was in big trouble.

Shayla stood in the center of the large kitchen, her heart hammering, her body quivering. She wasn't mistaken. Ian had thought about kissing her. If she hadn't turned away, he might have done it.

Letting herself care for this hunk of a cowboy had heartbreak written all over it. Did she want to be a substitute for the woman he'd once loved? No. She'd been settling for second best for far too many years. She'd been taking care of the needs of others for most of her life. Now it was *her* turn. *Hers!*

Oh, but she'd wanted his kisses. She'd wanted to step up close to him, press herself against his body and melt into his embrace. She'd wanted…

Leave now, she cautioned herself. *Get out while you still can.*

But her feet felt as if they'd been nailed to the floor. She couldn't move, couldn't run.

Now what?

Dear Reader,

Summer is a time for backyard barbecues and fun family gatherings. But with all the running around you'll be doing, don't forget to make time for yourself. And there's no better way to escape than with a Special Edition novel. Each month we offer six brand-new romances about people just like you—trying to find the perfect balance between life, career, family, romance....

To start, pick up *Hunter's Woman* by bestselling author Lindsay McKenna. Continuing her riveting MORGAN'S MERCENARIES: THE HUNTERS series, she pairs a strong-willed THAT SPECIAL WOMAN! with the ruggedly handsome soldier who loved her once—and is determined to win her back!

Every woman longs to be noticed for her true beauty—and the heroine of Joan Elliott Pickart's latest book, *The Irresistible Mr. Sinclair,* is no different; this novel features another wonderful hero in the author's exciting cross-line miniseries with Silhouette Desire, THE BACHELOR BET. And for those hankering to return to the beloved Western land that Myrna Temte takes us to in her HEARTS OF WYOMING series, don't miss *The Gal Who Took the West.*

And it's family that brings the next three couples together—a baby on the way in *Penny Parker's Pregnant!* by Stella Bagwell, the next installment in her TWINS ON THE DOORSTEP series that began in Silhouette Romance and will return there in January 2000; adorable twins in Robin Lee Hatcher's *Taking Care of the Twins;* and a millionaire's heir-to-be in talented new author Teresa Carpenter's *The Baby Due Date.*

I hope you enjoy these six emotional must-reads written *by* women like you, *for* women like you!

Sincerely,

Karen Taylor Richman
Senior Editor

Please address questions and book requests to:
Silhouette Reader Service
U.S.: 3010 Walden Ave., P.O. Box 1325, Buffalo, NY 14269
Canadian: P.O. Box 609, Fort Erie, Ont. L2A 5X3

ROBIN LEE HATCHER

TAKING CARE OF THE TWINS

Silhouette®

SPECIAL EDITION®

Published by Silhouette Books

America's Publisher of Contemporary Romance

To Ian, Shayla and Vince—my delightful trio of
grandchildren. You bring sunshine to my life.

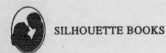 SILHOUETTE BOOKS

ISBN 0-373-24259-X

TAKING CARE OF THE TWINS

Visit us at www.romance.net

Printed in U.S.A.

Books by Robin Lee Hatcher

Silhouette Special Edition

Hometown Girl #1229
Taking Care of the Twins #1259

ROBIN LEE HATCHER

discovered her vocation as a writer after many years of reading everything she could put her hands on, including the backs of cereal boxes and ketchup bottles. However, she's certain there are better plots and fewer calories in her books than in puffed rice and hamburgers. A past president of Romance Writers of America, Robin is the author of over twenty-five novels. Her books have won numerous awards, including the Heart of Romance Readers' Choice Award for Best Historical, a Career Achievement Award for American Romance from *Romantic Times Magazine,* and the Favorite Historical Author Award from *Affaire de Coeur*. She was a finalist for the prestigious RWA RITA Award in 1992. For her efforts on behalf of literacy, Laubach Literacy International named their romance award "The Robin."

In those rare moments when she isn't working on a new book, Robin and her husband, Jerry, like to escape to their cabin in the mountains of Idaho with their border collie and Shetland sheepdog. Hobbies are nearly nonexistent since she sold her first book, but she enjoys the occasional golf game (don't ask about scores!), loves movies (both old and new) and live musical theater and is a season ticket holder with the Idaho Shakespeare Festival. She also loves to spend time with her two daughters and three young grandchildren. She invites readers to find out more by sending a #10 SASE to P.O. Box 4722, Boise, ID 83711-4722.

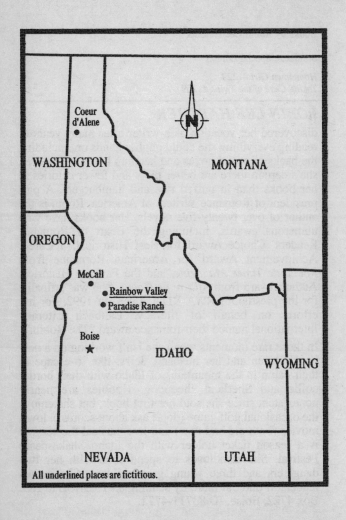

Coeur
d'Alene

WASHINGTON

MONTANA

OREGON

McCall

Rainbow Valley
Paradise Ranch

Boise

IDAHO

WYOMING

NEVADA

UTAH

All underlined places are fictitious.

Chapter One

Ian O'Connell knew almost everyone in Rainbow Valley, having lived there all his life, but he hadn't been introduced to his new neighbor, Shayla Vincent. And as he watched the petite young woman pacing back and forth across the dilapidated deck of the old Erickson cabin, muttering to herself and stabbing the air with a huge butcher knife, he wasn't sure he *wanted* to meet her.

Was she rehearsing a murder? That's what it looked like to him.

Common sense demanded that he turn Blue around and ride back to the ranch house. Curiosity made him stay. Besides, how dangerous could she be? She might be as mad as a March hare, but she couldn't outrun his horse.

She paused, shouted some words he couldn't quite

make out, then switched the knife to her left hand and thrust it through the air again.

Ian had known some screwball people in his life, but this gal beat anything he'd ever laid eyes on.

Suddenly she turned the blade's point toward herself, holding the hilt with both hands. Then she yanked it into her chest. With a painful cry, she fell backward onto the porch where she lay perfectly still.

"What the heck!"

Ian dug his heels into the gelding's sides and rode forward at a gallop. He vaulted to the ground even as Blue slid to a halt in front of the cabin.

The woman sat straight up before Ian's boots hit the first step. Her eyes widened as she squealed in alarm. "Who are you?" she demanded, jumping to her feet, obviously unharmed. The butcher knife clattered to the deck. "What do you want?" Her gaze darted to the knife, then back to him.

Her fearful questions brought Ian to an abrupt halt. He could tell she was weighing the risk of grabbing for the dropped weapon. There was no doubt in his mind that, frightened or not, she would use it if she had to.

"It's okay." He raised his hands in a gesture of acquiescence. "I thought you were hurt. I just wanted to help."

She didn't look quite as crazy now as she had a few moments before. Odd, maybe, in her oversize, bright purple-and-yellow tie-dyed T-shirt, her cutoff jeans with the frayed hems and her curly brown hair pulled into a bushy ponytail. Odd, but not crazy.

"Are you Miss Vincent? Shayla Vincent?"

Wariness remained in her dark blue eyes as she replied, "Yes. Why do you ask?"

"I saw your notice over at the Rainbow Laundromat.

For secretarial or housekeeping work? That's why I came to see you.''

''You're looking for an experienced secretary?'' She seemed to relax a little.

''No, a housekeeper.'' Cautiously he stepped up onto the deck and offered his hand. ''I'm Ian O'Connell. I own Paradise Ranch.''

She shook his proffered hand. Her grip was surprisingly firm for such a tiny gal.

''Then, I guess that makes us neighbors.''

He nodded. ''That it does.''

She observed him in silence a moment longer, then released his hand and said, ''I must be honest with you, Mr. O'Connell. The only reason I'm looking for work is so I can afford to make repairs to my cabin. Once they're done, I'll give my notice. I came from Portland to write a novel, not to clean other people's houses.''

''You're a writer?''

She nodded, then smiled wryly. ''Well, I hope to be. I've just started my first book. It's a murder mystery.''

Understanding dawned, and Ian chuckled.

''It isn't *that* preposterous, Mr. O'Connell.'' Her smile turned to a scowl. ''I *can* write, I assure you.''

''I'm sorry.'' He tried to look serious, but he was certain he failed. Quickly he added, ''I wasn't laughing because I thought you couldn't *be* a writer. It was…well…when I saw you stab yourself, I thought you might be…'' He tried to think of a polite word for insane—loco, crazy, nuts. Nothing came to him that seemed any better, so he let it drop. ''Anyway, now I think I understand what you were doing with that knife.''

Obviously seeing the humor in the scene he was describing, she smiled again. ''I guess it must have looked kind of weird at that. I was trying to figure out the angle of the entry wound. It all depends on how tall my murderer is and how short the victim.'' She picked up her weapon. ''It's a trick knife. It's got a retractable plastic blade. See? It's harmless.''

Definitely odd, he thought as he watched her demonstrate how the knife worked. But cute, too.

Shayla pointed with the blade toward a wooden bench. ''Would you like to sit down while we talk about your job offer?''

''Happy to oblige.'' He took a step forward, then stopped and glanced over his shoulder at her. ''I just had a thought. Would you be interested in trading services? At least for part of your wages? I'm a good carpenter and plumber, and I guarantee I can get to it quicker than the guys in town. They're always running behind.''

It would sure help his cash flow if she agreed to this plan. He needed a housekeeper, but ready cash didn't always keep regular company with a rancher.

''In fact,'' he continued as he settled onto the bench, ''I built those cabinets in the kitchen, and I was going to patch the roof. But then Miss Lauretta moved away. The place has been empty ever since. I didn't know it was up for sale.''

''It wasn't for sale. I'm Lauretta Erickson's niece.''

That explained a lot. Miss Lauretta was a strange one herself.

''Her great-niece, actually. Aunt Lauretta was my grandmother's younger sister.''

''Was?''

''She passed away this spring.''

''I'm sorry. I hadn't heard. She was a nice old lady. I liked her a lot.''

''She was the best.'' Shayla looked up, toward the cedar shake roof of the cabin. ''She left me this place in her will. Only, I remembered it as being in a whole lot better shape than it is now. Of course, it's been twenty-some years since I was here for a visit. I was about seven or eight, so maybe I just didn't notice the things that were wrong.'' She shook her head slowly. ''I wish I'd come again before she was forced to move away. She loved it here. I wish I'd...'' She let her words drift into silence as her eyes suddenly filled with tears.

Ian didn't say anything. He knew firsthand about losing someone you love. The hurt didn't go away overnight. It took time.

Sometimes it took years.

Shayla turned her back toward Ian O'Connell, not wanting a stranger to see her tears. She didn't want him feeling sorry for her or thinking she was weak or a crybaby.

But it was hard not to cry when she thought about Aunt Lauretta being gone for good. Even though they'd never lived in the same state—or seen each other often through the years—she and her great-aunt had shared a special bond, a unique understanding of one another. Aunt Lauretta was the only family member who hadn't told her she needed to be sensible and responsible. Her aunt had encouraged Shayla to follow her dreams, to take chances in life.

Until this spring, she hadn't tried to follow that advice. It had always seemed too impossible, something completely out of her reach. Moving away from her family. Writing a novel. Crazy ideas that were doomed to fail.

But because of Aunt Lauretta, she'd been given a real chance. She wasn't going to waste it. If only for her aunt's sake, she wasn't going to waste it.

Her neighbor cleared his throat. "Maybe I should come back later."

"No." She mentally pushed away her sadness. "No, Mr. O'Connell, I'd like to get this settled now if we can. I really do need a job. I've got to make repairs to this place before winter rolls around, but my funds are limited." She waved a hand toward the cabin. "You probably have a good idea why I need the extra cash if you did work for my aunt in the past."

He smiled. "Yeah, there's plenty that needs done around here."

For a moment, Shayla forgot the leaky places in the roof, the toilet that overflowed with wretched regularity, the faulty lock on the back door and the woodstove that didn't draw right. She couldn't think of anything except Ian's smile. It was absolutely charming, complete with dimples and one slightly crooked tooth.

And the rest of the Ian O'Connell package wasn't bad, either. He was tall and lean, tanned and muscular. His thick black hair was disheveled from the cowboy hat he'd removed earlier, hair that begged for a woman to smooth it with her fingertips. His brown eyes were the color of strong coffee, almost black, and the outer corners crinkled when he smiled, which he seemed to do often.

"Maybe I should tell you what I need from a housekeeper, Miss Vincent. It won't be easy work."

She suddenly remembered her own appearance. Most of her clothes were in the hamper, awaiting a trip to the Rainbow Laundromat. When she'd dressed that morning, she'd laughed about the awful T-shirt she was wearing, then thought, Who cares? Who will see me? The memory made her want to groan.

Here she was with Mr. Charming Smile himself, and

she was dressed like a bag lady, wearing no makeup, with her kinky-curly mop of mousy brown hair caught in a scrunchy atop her head, no doubt sticking out in all directions, as usual.

She felt a flush of embarrassment rushing into her cheeks. No wonder he'd thought her crazy.

Ian seemed unaware of her private agony. "I'd need you to come in for a few hours every day at first. I haven't had a housekeeper in more than a year, and the place is in pretty sad shape." He paused, grinning sheepishly. "I guess that'd be an understatement." Then he shrugged. "I'm a cattle rancher, and there's always plenty going on that needs my attention, always other things to spend my time and money on, if you know what I mean. I just never give much thought to the house, living alone like I do."

He lived alone. That was hard to believe. There must be something wrong with the women in this valley—or something wrong with him. She wondered which it was.

"My mother's been talking about coming for a visit later this summer," he continued. "If she sees it like it is right now, she'll skin me alive. She always took great pride in a tidy, well-run house."

Shayla nodded. She'd seen the enormous O'Connell ranch house from the highway. It looked more like a log castle than a mere home. She knew a place like that had to be spectacular on the inside and, sight unseen, could easily understand a woman taking pride in it.

"Once the deep down cleaning's done and things are organized properly again, I imagine you could keep things up pretty easily. Maybe come over once or twice a week, a few hours each time."

"You said you live alone. What about the men who work for you?" The last thing she wanted was to be cleaning up after a bunch of guys. She'd had enough of that when she lived with her parents and six younger siblings.

"Nope. My ranch hands don't bunk there. They've got their own homes and families to go to. Like I said, it's just me."

"No cooking," she said firmly.

"No cooking." That charming grin returned. "And no windows, either."

"And this trade in services would mean you'd do what around here?"

He put the Stetson on his head as he stood. "Well, we both know the roof needs patching. Why don't you show me around so we can figure out what else needs to be done and what needs attention first?"

"Sure. Come on in."

Half an hour later, Shayla watched from her deck as Ian mounted his dappled-gray horse. He made it look easy, sliding the toe of his boot into the stirrup, then stepping up and swinging his other leg over the saddle in one fluid movement. She'd never seen anything that looked so downright masculine and sexy in all her life.

She smiled to herself as she savored the view. Men who looked like him were undoubtedly why country music, Western novels and cowboy movies remained popular.

Hmm, she thought, worrying her lower lip with her teeth. Cowboys *were* popular. Maybe the protagonist in her book should be a rancher. With just a bit of tweaking, it might work. A cowboy sleuth. Had that ever been done in a mystery novel before? It would make sense.

All the how-to-write books said to write what you know. She was already using this valley and her cabin as the setting for her book. Instead of a small-town sheriff solving the murder, she could have her lead character be a cattle rancher with a really charming smile and dark hair and a lean body. A cowboy in tight Levi's and boots and—

"See you this afternoon," Ian said as he bent the brim of his hat between index finger and thumb in what she thought must be true cowboy fashion.

Oh, yes. She thought that would work. Male readers would like the rough, tough qualities of a cowboy, the man against nature, heap-big-hunter thing. And female readers would be drawn to that smile and his lean rugged look.

Absentmindedly, she replied, "I'll be there around two."

She turned and hurried inside, making a beeline for her computer. If she could just get down a few of these ideas before they disappeared. It wouldn't take her long at all. After that, she could change her clothes and go over to the O'Connell ranch.

Ian checked the anniversary clock on the mantel. It was almost three o'clock, and still no sign of Miss Vincent. She couldn't be lost. Her property bordered Paradise Ranch. All she had to do was take the dirt road to the highway, head south, then turn into the well-marked driveway. True, the driveway was two miles long, but it wasn't as if she couldn't *see* the big house from the road, set as it was on the hillside.

He frowned. Maybe she'd had a flat tire. Or maybe she'd had an accident. There were some bad boards in that deck of hers. If she'd broken through one of them, she could be lying there, helpless. If she had no telephone, as he suspected, she couldn't call for help if something was wrong.

He'd just about convinced himself to go looking for her when he heard the whine of a compact car's engine as it raced into the yard. A moment later, a cloud of dust whirled past his living room window. Then he heard the slam of a car door.

He stepped onto the porch in time to see Shayla checking her reflection in the side-view mirror. And an attractive reflection it was, too. Unconventional, perhaps, but appealing.

She'd applied some makeup before coming over— shadow and mascara to her eyes, pink lipstick to her mouth—and her wild curls had been tamed a little, though not much. She'd changed from her extra large T-shirt and frayed cutoffs into a silvery-gray blouse and a pair of jeans that showed off more of her figure than he'd noticed earlier. And a nice figure it was. Shayla was curvaceous in all the right places. He'd bet she would fit real nicely in a man's arms.

Get a grip, O'Connell. She's not your type.

She straightened, and that's when she noticed him watching her. Twin patches of pink dotted her cheeks. "Sorry I'm late."

"Car trouble?"

"No." She grew more flushed. "I lost track of the time. That happens to me when I'm writing. I get so involved in the story that I forget to look at the clock."

At least she hadn't tried to make up an excuse or sound like it wasn't her own fault. He appreciated honesty.

"I would've called once I saw the time, but my phone isn't working yet." She walked toward him. "The phone company told me it wouldn't be until week after next.

Why it takes so long I'll never understand. Aunt Lauretta had a phone. The place doesn't have to be wired or anything."

"Things move a bit slow around here."

"Me included." She revealed an apologetic grin. "I *am* truly sorry for making you wait."

"No problem." He was the one not being honest. It *was* a problem. He had a dozen unfinished chores that had to be done yet today. "Come inside and see what you're getting yourself into." He held open the door and waited while she passed by him.

She paused on the parquet entry. "Wow!"

He didn't know if her one-word exclamation referred to the design of the house or the clutter and disorder she could see everywhere. He preferred to think it was the former.

"How long have you lived here?" she asked.

"All my life. I was born in one of the bedrooms upstairs. Doctor got here about ten minutes after I did. Or so my mother likes to tell folks every chance she gets."

"Really? How interesting. Hmm…"

Ian couldn't help noticing the way her eyes seemed to glaze over. He had the distinct feeling she was no longer with him, even though he could still see her. "Miss Vincent?"

"Chet's mother…." She pursed her lips and nodded as she looked up the staircase. Then she whispered, "Of course. How perfect."

Oh, brother. Now she was talking to herself.

"Miss Vincent?" he said again, louder this time.

She blinked, shook her head, looked at him. "Yes?"

"Let me show you around. Maybe, after you see what a disaster it is, you'll decide you don't want the job." At this point, he didn't know if that's what he hoped for or not. He needed someone he could depend upon. He wasn't convinced that someone was her.

"Good idea," she responded. "I'm dying to see it." She looked toward the room to their right.

A good idea? Maybe. Maybe not. But he had little choice except to follow through with it now. "My mother called this the great room." He motioned for her to enter ahead of him.

A stone fireplace was the focal point of the oversize room. An oil painting of Rainbow Valley as it had looked in the early 1900s hung above the mantel, and like many others before her, Shayla was drawn toward it.

"O'Connell," she said, reading the signature in the bottom right corner. She glanced over her shoulder. "Did *you* do this? It's magnificent."

"No." His answer was clipped. "I don't paint." Even after ten years, he found it uncomfortable to talk about Joanne and her art.

Shayla continued to look at him, waiting for him to fully answer her question. He figured she was the type who would wait as long as it took.

Steeling himself, he said, "My wife painted it."

"Your wife?" She fully faced him, her eyes wide. "But I thought you said—"

"She's dead."

"Oh, I'm so sorry. I didn't—"

"It happened years ago." He turned abruptly. "The library is this way."

Shayla hesitated a moment before following him, wishing she knew what to say. But then, she supposed it was better to say nothing since that's what he seemed to want.

"Are you coming, Miss Vincent?"

"Yes." She hurried to catch up with him, hoping she wouldn't make any more blunders.

While Ian showed her the library, his office and the sitting room, Shayla confined herself to brief murmurs of appreciation. But when Ian led her into the huge kitchen, she couldn't stay silent any longer.

"Oh my! This is incredible."

The room had a bank of windows on two sides. Stainless-steel counters and sinks gleamed in the afternoon sunlight. Pots and pans and other cookware hung from hooks in the tall ceiling above a center island. There were six burners on the stove and two ovens, and the refrigerator was large enough to walk into.

"It looks like a restaurant."

"My grandma cooked for a lot of ranch hands back in the early years, back when Paradise Ranch was all that was in this valley. 'Course, the kitchen didn't always look like it does now. Started out with a woodstove and an icebox and a plain wood floor. It's been remodeled a time or two since then, but it was always this big."

Shayla slowly walked around the room, running her fingers over the countertops, admiring the details. Even the need for a thorough cleaning couldn't diminish the wonder of it.

"What my mother wouldn't have given for a kitchen like this," she said. "There were seven of us kids, and we were always underfoot when Mom was trying to cook."

"Seven kids?"

"Seven. I've got three brothers and three sisters." She pictured them in her mind, playing and fighting the way they'd done throughout the years. She'd come to Idaho, in part, to get away from her large, ofttimes demanding family, and yet she still missed them.

"And which number are you?"

"I'm the oldest." She turned toward him. "What about you?"

"Just one older sister. Leigh. She and Jim, her husband, live in Florida with their twin daughters. My mother lives near them." He looked out the windows toward the pine-covered mountains that rose from his backyard. "We're all that's left of the O'Connell family now. My grandparents are gone, and my dad died about eight years ago."

She thought he looked lonely and wondered if he continued to mourn the wife he'd lost.

Still gazing out the window, he continued. "I always thought this ranch ought to be crawling with kids. But Joanne and I never...." He didn't finish the sentence.

Shayla remembered her less-than-congenial words of farewell to her mom and dad before leaving Portland. She'd essentially told them she was sick to death of her brothers and sisters, and she didn't care if she never saw any of them ever again.

She shouldn't have said it. She loved her family. She'd simply been fed up with being the big sister and had said things she didn't mean because of her anger and frustration.

But she also believed that this was her one and only chance to grab for the brass ring. Thanks to Aunt Lauretta's legacy, she had about one year to chase after her dream. One year. Twelve precious months. If she didn't do it now, if she didn't at least *try* now, she never would.

"Let's move on to the upstairs," Ian said, interrupting her thoughts. "After you see the mess up there, you still might decide against taking the job."

She had to make repairs to the cabin so she could live and work there during the upcoming winter. She had to write her book. She couldn't allow herself to fail. She couldn't go back to being what she'd always been. A nobody on the road to nowhere. At most, just someone's big sister.

Firmly she said, "I'm not going to change my mind, Mr. O'Connell. You can bet on that."

Chapter Two

Hunkering down, Chet touched the tire tracks with his fingers. It had rained last night, and the ground had been soft and muddy. The grooves were deep, as could be expected from heavy trucks full of cattle.

Trucks full of Eden Ranch *cattle.*

It had been Neal Goodman's hard luck to stumble upon the rustlers in action. Now Chet's good friend and ranch foreman lay on a slab in the morgue, and a hundred head of Morrison cattle were missing. In the meantime, the sheriff was busy playing politics instead of trying to find the men responsible.

He frowned as he stood, sweeping the area with his gaze, looking for clues. Whoever had done this had known where the cattle would be yesterday. The rustlers hadn't just chanced to pick Eden Ranch. They'd planned the operation carefully. They'd known about the cattle drive up to the north range.

Whoever killed Neal was someone who knew both the foreman and Chet. Someone Chet might still call a friend.

He gritted his teeth at the thought.

Well, maybe while Sheriff Tuttle was writing his speech for the Eden Valley Ladies' Quilting Club, Chet would take care of the matter himself. Nobody caused trouble on Eden Ranch and got away with it. Not as long as he had any say in it, they didn't.

Not even a so-called friend.

Shayla leaned back in her chair and tapped her index finger against her chin while reading the last few paragraphs. Poor Neal. She'd grown rather fond of Chet's ranch foreman. But somebody from Eden Ranch had to die at this point in the story, and Neal had been the logical character to go.

So now what was Chet, her cowboy/amateur detective, going to do about it?

She rolled her chair back from her computer desk, rose and walked outside. Through the pines and aspens, she could see Paradise cattle grazing in knee-high grass.

Hmm. Chet's cattle had been stolen. How hard was it to round up a bunch of them? No, not a bunch. A herd. So how difficult could it be? And how many trucks would be needed to haul out a hundred of them?

She descended the steps and strolled down the short drive, across the dusty country road and up to the barbed-wire fence that marked the border of O'Connell land.

"No gate. They'd have to snip the wire. Then they could back their trucks up to the opening. That would work...but I don't want more than two or three men involved. Somebody could talk...." She scrunched up her mouth, deep in thought. "Dogs. They could use dogs to help them, I'll bet. But what breed of dog?" She glanced at the reddish brown-and-white cattle again. "And what kind of cows are those?"

Ian could answer her questions.

The image of her handsome neighbor popped into her head. Something told her that he wouldn't be flattered to know he was the model for the protagonist of her murder mystery, although she couldn't say why. Still, she didn't think he'd mind if she asked him a few questions about a rancher's life.

She glanced up. Judging by the sun, it was about noon. Maybe Ian would be on his lunch break. It seemed silly to wait until Monday, when she was scheduled to start work at his place. She needed answers now so she could keep writing.

Besides, she could use some exercise. A brisk walk would do her good.

That decided, she carefully held open two strands of barbed wire and managed to slip through without snagging either her shirt or her shorts. Then she headed across the pasture, giving the grazing cattle a wide berth.

The rugged mountains that surrounded this long, wide valley—mountains perfectly described by the words *purple majesty*—still wore a frosting of snow on their highest peaks, despite the warm days of early June. Here in their shadow, wildflowers blanketed the valley floor, purple and white and yellow amidst a sea of yellow-green. The long grass whispered as it waved in a gentle breeze. In the distance, she could hear the whine of a truck engine, a lonesome sound in the otherwise quiet day.

But Shayla didn't feel lonely. She liked the solitude.

She liked everything about Rainbow Valley. She couldn't imagine anyone not liking it.

"Thanks, Aunt Lauretta," she whispered.

If it weren't for her great-aunt, she would still be living in Portland, probably stuck in another dead-end job, her writing dreams still on hold, unrealized.

She remembered the expression on her sister Anne's face when she'd announced her intention of moving to Idaho to write a mystery novel.

"Write a novel?" Anne had exclaimed. "Why would you want to do that?"

And Anne hadn't been the only one who'd reacted that way. It was as if Shayla had never before mentioned her desire to write. All her brothers and sisters thought her crazy for leaving Portland and moving to this remote area. Her parents, too. None of them understood. Perhaps because none of them seemed to know she might want a life of her own.

"Shouldn't you just sell that old cabin?" her mother had asked. "It must be worth something. I know you're discouraged about losing your job. Twelve years is a long time with one employer. But there must be something better for you to do than move to Idaho and fritter away the money Aunt Lauretta left you. You're an excellent secretary, Shayla. You'll find another position. You haven't even tried. You could move home until then. That would save money."

Shayla stopped walking and, for a moment, stood perfectly still, eyes closed, simply breathing in and out while telling herself not to be hurt and angered by her family's lack of understanding. She knew they didn't mean to be thoughtless or to hurt her feelings. She knew they loved her. Still, it would be nice if, just once, they…

A strange sound intruded on her thoughts.

She opened her eyes—and discovered an enormous bull staring back at her from about twenty-five yards away. The animal was complete with a ring in its nose, wicked-looking horns and eyes that promised physical harm to whatever stood in its path.

She was in its path.

The bull pawed the ground, snorting, nostrils flared, and she knew in that instant that her time on earth was about to end. What a horrible way to die.

And then she was suddenly airborne.

"Darn fool!" a male voice shouted above the thunder of galloping hooves.

She would have replied, only she was helpless to do so. Her rescuer's arm was wrapped tightly around her stomach, making it hard to draw a breath, let alone speak. Bent at the waist, staring at the ground speeding by beneath her, she bounced against the man's thigh and the side of the horse as they raced across the pasture.

It seemed an eternity before the horse came to a halt, and Shayla was half lowered, half dropped to the ground.

"What were you thinking?"

Breathless, she looked up into Ian's glowering eyes. "I...I..." she gasped, helpless to say anything else.

He swung down from the saddle. "You're lucky Satan didn't kill you."

Satan? Oh my. Her legs gave out, and she sat down with a soft thud.

"Hey, you okay?" He didn't sound quite as angry as before.

"Yes, I'm okay. Just...just a bit frightened."

"With good reason. That was a darn fool stunt to pull." He knelt down in front of her. "Don't you pay attention to No Trespassing signs?"

"I...I didn't see any signs."

He raised an eyebrow. "How could you not? They're all along the fence you climbed over."

Climbed over?

She glanced behind her. Sure enough, there was a white board fence. She didn't remember either seeing it or climbing over it, but she must have done so. How else could she have…?

"Hey." Ian's fingers squeezed her shoulder. "You'd better put your head between your knees. You look like you're gonna pass out."

"Don't be silly. I've never fa—"

Blackness swallowed her whole.

Ian lifted Shayla into his arms and strode toward the house. His gelding followed behind of his own accord.

"Flatlanders ought to stay in the city where they belong," Ian muttered. "Right, Blue?"

The horse snorted, as if in agreement.

"Darn fool female."

Again a snort of agreement.

She was easy to carry, even in a dead faint. Probably didn't weigh more than a hundred, maybe a hundred and five pounds. And she fit nicely against him. Between carrying her or stacking hay bales, as he'd been doing all morning, he'd choose carrying Shayla Vincent any day of the week.

He glanced down at the woman in his arms. She was cute, in her own unusual fashion. Soft in all the right places, too.

Whoa, O'Connell! he thought. Back up the buckboard.

This city gal wasn't going to make it through one central Idaho winter. By the time the snow was five feet deep outside the front door of that cabin, the little mystery writer would have hightailed it back to Oregon. And that was as it should be.

Besides, he didn't care how cute his neighbor was. When he got interested in a female again, it was going to be with one who wanted to spend the rest of her days in this valley, living and working right alongside him, one who didn't mind being snowbound for several months each winter, one who wanted the same things he wanted.

The trouble was how to find a woman like that. He'd thought Joanne fit the bill. He'd thought they wanted the same things—this ranch, a houseful of kids, a simple way of life. But he'd been wrong.

He shook off the unpleasant memories as he climbed the steps to the veranda.

After entering the house, he carried Shayla into the great room. She started to come to just as he laid her on the couch.

"What happened?" she asked softly, looking up at him with confused eyes.

"You fainted."

"Don't be silly."

"I think those were your exact words before you passed out."

She pushed herself upright.

"I suppose you don't remember your close encounter with Satan, either."

"Satan?" Her eyes widened, then she lay down with a groan. "Oh, yes. Satan." The color drained from her face a second time. Her eyes fluttered closed.

"Hey. Stay with me." He took hold of her hand. "Miss Vincent. Look at me."

She obeyed with obvious effort. "You shouldn't keep such a dangerous creature. Somebody could get hurt."

"Seems to me that's why I put up those signs you didn't see. Besides, this *is* a cattle ranch. What did you expect to find? Little lambs?"

"You're right." She groaned again. "Guilty as charged."

He stifled a grin. "You still look a bit green around the gills. Lie quiet while I get you a glass of water. Maybe it'll help."

As he walked away, he heard her feeble "Thanks."

Shayla wished she could simply disappear. She'd never fainted in her life. In her not-so-humble opinion, swooning females were an embarrassment to their gender. She could just imagine what her hunk of a cowboy neighbor thought of her now. Not that it should matter to her.

The image of that angry, snorting, pawing bull returned in a rush. She could almost feel its hot breath on her skin. She could almost feel those horns piercing her flesh.

The blood drained from her head, and she closed her eyes again.

"Here you go," she heard Ian saying as he returned to the room.

"He would have killed me, wouldn't he? That bull." She opened her eyes. "Satan."

"He might have tried." He held out the glass of water. "He's plenty mean. I probably should haul him off to market, but he's the best bull Paradise ever had. Just can't make myself get rid of him now that he's past his prime."

Slowly she sat up. When it seemed she was going to stay upright this time, she took the glass from him. "Just how big is he? He looked enormous."

"He weighs in at about twenty-two hundred pounds. About the max for a Hereford."

She gulped, envisioning the bull's pointed horns and its evil eyes.

"Never been on a working ranch before, have you?"

"Not really." She took a sip of water.

"Well, then, there's a few things you probably oughta know." He sat on a nearby chair. "First lesson, read what's posted. Think of the signs you find on fences and gates like traffic signs at a busy intersection. Run a stop, and you're likely to get hit by something coming the other direction."

"I'll remember that."

"Good." He smiled.

She forgot the old bull. She forgot what she was doing there.

"So tell me a little about your life in the city. Portland, was it?"

"Yes." She sounded out of breath, even to herself. She took another sip of water, giving herself a moment to regroup. "What would you like to know?"

"Well, start with how long you lived there."

"All my life. My parents, too."

"How about your brothers and sisters? Do they all live in Portland?"

"Yes, and three of them are still at home. Crystal's the youngest. She's thirteen."

"I always wanted to be part of a big family."

Shayla shook her head. "Believe me, it isn't all it's cracked up to be." She hadn't meant to sound sarcastic, but she knew she had.

He watched her with those intent, dark eyes of his. She wondered if he would ask her more about her family and wasn't sure if she was relieved or not when he didn't.

"Feeling better?"

She set down the water glass and rose from the sofa. "Yes. I should start for home. By the long route this time."

He stood, too. "You never told me what you were doing out there in the middle of that paddock. I assume you were on your way to see me about something."

"It wasn't important." To be honest, she couldn't remember why she'd come. Not with him watching her that way.

"You didn't change your mind about working for me, did you?" He looked worried.

"No, I definitely am *not* changing my mind about that." She thought of her parents and siblings, all of them expecting her to fail.

He didn't press for any further explanation. "I'll give you a lift home."

"Thanks, but you don't need to."

"I know that. I *want* to. You still look a tad pale."

Embarrassed by the reminder, she acquiesced with a nod. "All right."

He motioned with his hand for her to follow him, then headed toward the kitchen, leading her through it and out the back door. A newer-model, teal-colored pickup was parked in the shade of a tall, leafy tree.

Ian let out a sharp, short whistle as he strode toward the vehicle. Seconds later, two black-and-white dogs came racing across the barnyard and jumped into the truck bed. "Hey, girls." He reached over the side of the truck and patted their heads. To Shayla, he said, "Meet Bonny and Coira."

"They're beautiful. What kind are they?"

"Border collies. Smartest cow dog there is, far as I'm concerned."

Her earlier questions—the ones that had brought her to Paradise Ranch—came rushing back. Ian had answered a couple of them without her even asking. He raised Herefords and his dogs were border collies. Now she wanted to know more.

"So, could a couple of dogs like these two help a man round up a herd of cows?" She stroked Bonny's head as she spoke. "Even at night in the dark?"

"Piece of cake."

"I'd love to see them work sometime."

"You'll have plenty of opportunity for that this summer." He moved around the truck to the passenger side and opened the door for her.

When was the last time a man had done something like that? Not counting her dad or her brothers. Not that they did it very often, either. To them, she was the capable, dependable daughter and sister, used to taking care of others rather than being taken care of herself.

As Ian helped her into the pickup, she thought about her last serious relationship. Gordon Sampson was a nice man with pleasant good looks. Gordon, a co-worker of her dad's, and his family had joined the Vincent clan for Fourth of July picnics and Christmas parties often through the years. After Dee Sampson deserted her husband and their two children, running off to Europe with another man, Gordon had come to the Vincent house more and more often, talking for hours with Shayla's mom and dad, seeking advice and comfort.

And then one day he'd asked Shayla out on a date. At first she'd been flattered. She'd never had an abundance of beaux. Not as a teenager in school nor as an adult. She wasn't tall or beautiful or any of the other things men seemed to like in a woman. So she'd agreed to go out with him. But after several months of dating, it had become painfully obvious to her that Gordon wasn't looking for a woman whom he could love but for a surrogate mother for his children. He needed a nanny, not a life partner.

"I've already helped raise my brothers and sisters," she'd told him the last time they were together. "I'm not taking on any more. I want a life of my own."

Her mother had recently written that Gordon had married again, a lovely young woman in her twenties who was already pregnant with their first child.

More power to her.

After starting the truck, Ian glanced at Shayla. She was deep in thought, and it was apparent those thoughts weren't entirely pleasant ones. A tiny frown had drawn her brows together, furrowing her forehead. Her blue eyes were clouded, troubled. She was worrying her lower lip between her teeth, something he'd seen her do several times since they'd first met.

She intrigued him, he realized as he drove out of the yard and toward the highway. He supposed that was because she was unlike anyone he'd known before. Most of the folks in this valley had lived there for many years. They were ranchers and cowboys or they worked for the highway department or forest service or they owned small businesses in town. They knew each others' names and the names of their kids and grandkids. And more often than not, they knew what the others liked for breakfast and the last time a neighbor had had a cold or the flu. A few lived in remote shacks farther up in the mountains, along old logging roads, their closest neighbors being mule deer, elk, bears, mountain lions and bobcats.

Shayla Vincent, on the other hand, was a city girl. She didn't have enough sense to know a colt from a filly, let alone enough to recognize the danger of strolling into a paddock with a cantankerous old bull. She didn't belong here, and she wouldn't last.

Even folks who *did* belong didn't always last.

He'd learned that the hard way.

Chapter Three

The redbrick community Christian church at the corner of Main and Second was well attended on this beautiful summer day. Prior to the start of the Sunday service, members of the congregation gathered on the sidewalk, enjoying the fresh morning breeze while visiting with their friends and neighbors, discussing the price of feed, the new tractor Owen Overstreet bought last week and the news that the youngest Paulson girl had left on the bus for New York City night before last, hoping to make a name for herself on Broadway.

Standing with a group of men on the Main Street side of the church, Ian saw Shayla climbing the steps to the church entrance. She wore a sleeveless dress, butter-yellow in color, that whispered in a soft fall of fabric around her calves. Her hair had been braided, the end caught with a satin bow. In her arms she carried a Bible.

He was a little surprised to see her at church, perhaps

because she hadn't come to services since moving to the valley.

He watched as she was welcomed by the pastor's wife, Geneve Barnett. The two women shook hands while exchanging a few words of introduction. Then Shayla moved through the open doorway, disappearing from view.

Ian excused himself from those around him and made his way inside, for some reason curious for another glimpse of his neighbor. It took his eyes a few moments to adjust from the bright daylight outside to the softer light of the sanctuary. After they did, he scanned the room until he found her. She'd taken a seat in the back pew beneath the balcony, a spot that blanketed her in shadows.

On purpose, he suspected.

She was an outsider from a big city. She had to feel out of place and maybe even a little bit lonely. Of course it wasn't his place to worry about her. She was an adult. She could make her own friends without his help.

And yet something propelled him forward and into that back pew.

"Morning, Shayla," he said as he removed his hat.

The instant their gazes met, she smiled. "Good morning, Ian."

"Nice to see you in church."

"Nice to be here, too."

"How are you today?"

"Do you mean, am I going to faint again?" She laughed softly, a pretty, almost musical sound. "I think I'm over that particular malady."

That wasn't what he'd meant, but he liked the way she could laugh at herself.

"Good," he replied. "No more fainting." He sat

down beside her, placing his Stetson on the floor beneath the pew.

Her eyes widened a fraction, revealing her surprise that he was joining her.

He didn't figure she was any more surprised than he was. He hadn't sat anyplace in this church except the third row, piano side, since he was knee-high to a grasshopper. That had been the O'Connell pew for more than sixty years, first for his grandparents, then for his parents and finally for Ian.

And Joanne, too, before she died.

It had been ten years since he'd sat in the O'Connell pew with his wife by his side, many years longer since there'd been any kids there, whispering and getting dirty looks from their mother. That wasn't how it was supposed to have turned out, but that's the way it was.

"It's a lovely old church, isn't it?" Shayla said softly.

He shook off his unsettling memories and answered, "Yeah. My granddad helped build it after the original wooden building burned down. Hauled the bricks up from Boise in a freight wagon back during the Depression."

"Your roots go down deep, don't they?"

He nodded. "Real deep."

The organist began to play, intruding on their conversation.

Leaning closer, Shayla whispered, "I'd like to hear more sometime. About how your family came to this valley, I mean." She shrugged. "It's the writer in me. I'm curious about everything."

He couldn't help wondering if he'd want her to be curious about him for some *other* reason besides her writing.

* * *

Rainbow Community Church had a splendid preacher in Roger Barnett, and Shayla enjoyed the worship service that morning. She particularly liked standing next to Ian and listening to his fine singing voice. There was a richness and depth in it that touched her heart.

It wasn't until the service concluded and people came over to meet her that she became aware she'd been the subject of much speculation during the previous hour. Then she realized they thought she was *with* Ian.

The notion was so preposterous, she nearly laughed aloud.

Men who looked like Ian didn't date women who looked like her. They chose those tall, lithe, gorgeous blondes or brunettes, the ones who resembled the models whose images adorned the covers of the magazines that filled those slots next to supermarket checkout lines. She hadn't reached the ripe old age of thirty without learning that lesson, and learning it well.

And it wasn't like it mattered to her, she thought a short while later as she drove toward home. She was comfortable enough with her appearance. She didn't mind as much as she used to that she was short and plump and rather ordinary looking.

Besides, she wasn't in the market for a man. She had no time for a relationship, serious or otherwise. She had other fish to fry, an expression her mom had been fond of using whenever her eldest daughter broke up with a guy—or got dumped. One day, the name Shayla Vincent would appear on the covers of books in stores, airports and on the Internet. That was what mattered most to her now.

But Ian *could* become a good friend. She'd like that, especially since she planned to live in these parts a long, long time. They *were* neighbors, after all. She was going to clean his kitchen and he was going to fix her roof. What better basis for two people to form a friendship?

At the cabin, she parked her fifteen-year-old car between two tamaracks, then went inside. She put her Bible on the coffee table, then switched on the radio to a country-western station before going into the bedroom to change out of her dress and into a T-shirt and pair of shorts. Afterward, she poured herself a glass of ice tea from the pitcher in the refrigerator, then went to sit on the deck.

She supposed she should do some work this afternoon. Tomorrow she'd probably be too tired to write after she returned from Paradise Ranch. What a mess she was about to tackle! She hadn't let on, of course, but it had been a while since she'd seen so much clutter and disorganization in one house. And Ian lived there alone.

If there was anything she'd learned as the oldest of seven children, all residing under one roof, it was how to keep things neat and tidy. Otherwise you lost the things that were yours.

Sipping her tea, she allowed her thoughts to drift to her family. Her parents, Doug and Reba Vincent, hadn't ever had much money, but they'd had plenty of love, especially for kids. Shayla had arrived the year after they were married. Eight years separated her and her brother, Dwight, but the rest of the Vincent children had followed in rapid succession. Anne, at twenty-one, was one year younger to the day than Dwight. Ken was twenty. Olivia had just turned seventeen this month. George would be fifteen in two weeks. And Crystal, the "baby" sister, was thirteen.

Shayla couldn't seem to remember a time when she hadn't been helping her mom change diapers or feed one baby or another. In fact, she'd postponed moving out on her own after graduating from high school because she was needed at home. There hadn't been enough money for full-time college, so she'd settled for taking the occasional night class while working as a secretary during the day.

And all the while, she'd harbored the dream of one day writing great novels. Sometimes, while still living with the family, she'd locked herself in the bathroom with a good book, just for a moment of peace and quiet to herself. She would read and think, *I could do this. I want to do this.*

She felt the sting of disappointment once again, wondering why no one had tried to understand her dreams and aspirations. Even when she moved into a place of her own, she hadn't found time to write. At least one of her brothers or sisters, several of them teenagers by that time, had been in the midst of a crisis at any given moment. Whenever that happened, they'd ended up at her apartment, bunking on her couch, bending her ear with their complaints, whining that no one understood them.

But no one had ever wanted to hear *her* complaints.

She set aside her empty glass and rose from the deck chair. She wasn't particularly happy about this recent habit of sinking into self-pity. She was on her own now. She'd been given her chance to do what *she* wanted to do. She simply had to make the best of it.

With that in mind, she headed inside to turn on her computer.

Ian was napping on the couch, taking advantage of his one day of rest, when the phone rang. It was his sister, Leigh.

"Sleeping, weren't you?" she said in response to his mumbled greeting.

"Yeah." He yawned, then asked, "What's up, sis? How are things in Florida?"

"Everyone here is great. Mom's having a bit of trouble with her hip again, but she says she can get along fine with a little discomfort."

"Has she decided when she's coming to Paradise for a visit?"

"I don't think so. You'd have to ask her. My guess is, it won't be until fall. She's got a pretty full summer planned with all her retiree friends."

He nodded. Their mother had never been one to sit idle for long.

"Listen, Ian.... The reason I called is I need a favor. A big one."

"I'll do what I can. You know that."

"Yes, I know."

When she didn't continue right away, he wondered just how big—how serious—this favor was going to be. He even felt a niggle of worry. Maybe something was wrong that she hadn't told him. Maybe their mom's hip problems were more serious than Leigh had let on. Maybe....

"Jim's firm is sending him to Saudi Arabia," she offered at last. "He'll be there from six months to a year."

"Wow!"

"It's a big promotion for him. A wonderful opportunity."

"But?"

"He wants me to go with him.... Only, we aren't allowed to take the girls." She paused a moment before saying, "I'd like to have Cathy and Angie stay with you at the ranch."

"Holy cow," he whispered.

"You know how great it was for us, growing up

there," she hurried to add. "And you *are* their only uncle. Mom couldn't possibly do it. For a week or two maybe, but not for up to a year. What do you say, Ian? Will you let them come live with you? Jim and I would pay for whatever childcare you would need to arrange when you aren't around."

"I don't know, Leigh. I don't have any experience with—"

"You always said you wanted a large family."

"Well, yes, but I thought I'd start from the ground up. You know. Get married first. Then have a baby."

"Ian, I'm desperate," Leigh said softly. "There isn't anyone else to ask. I can't put them in a boarding school. They would be too unhappy there. They're only six years old. They need to be with family, with someone who will love them. If you turn me down, I won't be able to go with Jim."

His sister was right. Paradise was the perfect place for the girls. They should experience living in the mountains. They should see how things worked on a ranch. They ought to live through one Idaho winter with tons of real snow instead of staying in the summerlike conditions of Florida. And how difficult could it be to take care of a couple of six year olds, anyway?

"Okay, Leigh. I'll do it. You knew I couldn't say no to you, didn't you?"

"Yes, I knew it," she said with a laugh. "But you had me worried for a second or two."

"So when should I plan for them to arrive?"

"Not for about a month. We have all sorts of things to work out first. We'll have to close the house and put things in storage." She lowered her voice. "Jim and I can't thank you enough for agreeing to do this for us. Really."

"No big deal. I'm glad to do it. And you're right—it'll be good practice for when I have kids of my own."

"I'll call you again in a few days. As soon as I can give you more details."

"Great."

"I love you, bro."

"Back atcha, sis."

"Talk to you soon."

"Sure thing."

After Ian placed the receiver in its cradle, he leaned back on the sofa and closed his eyes.

It'll be good practice for when I have kids of my own.

But when, if ever, was that going to happen?

He was thirty-five years old. Thirty-five, unmarried and not seeing anyone at the present.

The last woman he'd dated had been looking for a meal ticket, thinking anyone with a spread like Paradise had to be rolling in the dough. He'd set her straight, then sent her on her way in a hurry.

The woman before that had been special in many ways, but after several months of dating, they'd realized there was no spark between them, no excitement, no wanting more. They had been comfortable together and had enjoyed one another's company. But love wasn't going to happen and both had known it. So they'd gone their separate ways.

He could feel his hope for a large family of his own slipping beyond his grasp. It wasn't like there was an abundance of single women in Rainbow Valley, waiting for Ian to choose one of them to be his bride and bear his children.

He suddenly envisioned his slightly odd but definitely cute new neighbor, remembering at the same time the way she'd felt in his arms when he'd carried her into the house yesterday. And once again he reacted with surprise and denial. He could *never* be interested in her. Sure, she was nice enough, and he was glad to be neighborly.

But she wasn't his type. Pure and simple.

With smoke billowing out behind her, Shayla raced through the front door, carrying a blackened roast in its pot. Eyes watering and throat smarting, she tossed the ruined meat over the deck railing, dropped the pot and oven mitts onto the deck, then sank onto the top step, fighting the urge to dissolve into tears of frustration.

"Don't like well-done beef?"

She looked up to find Ian O'Connell leaning his hip against his pickup, his arms crossed over his chest. A half smile curved his mouth, and his eyes twinkled with amusement.

Well, it figured he would be there to see this. He usually showed up during her worst moments, didn't he?

"The oven overheated," she explained.

He pushed off the truck and strode toward her. "The whole place isn't going to burn down while we talk, is it?"

"No." She glanced over her shoulder. The smoke was beginning to clear. "But maybe it should," she added with a note of disgust.

"Why don't I check it out?"

"Be my guest." She didn't bother to rise. Merely slid over to one side so he could get past her.

One more thing needing repair. One more drain on the inheritance that had seemed bountiful when she'd received it but now seemed so inadequate. She could almost hear her mother saying, *Come home, dear, where you belong.*

She pressed the heels of her hands against her closed eyes, her elbows resting on her thighs. Why couldn't something go her way? Just for once!

"I opened the windows," Ian told her a short while later. He sat down on the step next to her. "It's the thermostat, I think. Or maybe the element. Shouldn't be too expensive to replace."

She straightened and looked toward him. "Even for a stove that old?"

"We'll get it fixed. Don't worry."

Don't worry. Easy for him to say.

"I'll run into town as soon as the hardware store opens in the morning. With luck, Ed will have the part in stock. Plenty of old stoves in this valley."

"You don't have to do that. If you just tell me what I need—"

"Glad to do it." He patted her shoulder and smiled. "And since you'll be busy cleaning my house all this next week, you sure aren't going to have time for it."

Her heart started doing a little soft-shoe routine in her chest, then burst into overdrive. Her body felt too warm, the heat radiating out from the place where his hand rested on her shoulder.

"Nearly forgot what brought me over." He straightened, removing his hand. "I was thinking this afternoon about you being in this cabin all by yourself and wondered if you might like some company."

Was he saying *he* wanted to be with her? Her pulse quickened even more.

"I've got some sheltie pups that are just weaned and thought you might like to have one."

Her romantic notions crashed into familiar disappointment. Of course. He was offering her a pet to be her companion, not himself. How could she have thought otherwise? Even for a millisecond.

"You like dogs, don't you?" he continued, oblivious to her thoughts.

"Yes, I like dogs."

"Good." He stood. "I brought one with me, just in case." He headed for the truck.

Shayla's sister Anne was the classic beauty in the family. If it was beautiful Anne living in this cabin, Ian wouldn't be bringing *her* a puppy for company. He'd be bringing flowers—and himself!

She clenched her teeth. She *had* to get off this pity-me kick. The last thing she had time for in her life was a man to mess it up.

She watched as Ian opened his truck door and reached inside. A few moments later, he returned to where she sat, carrying with him a little orange-and-white ball of fur with big golden brown eyes and a shiny black nose. Shayla couldn't help laughing as she accepted the quivering, tail-wagging, whimpering pup, her disappointment instantly forgotten.

"Oh, she's adorable." She met Ian's gaze. "Is it a she?"

"Yup."

"What's her name?" She rubbed her cheek against the puppy's soft coat.

"That's up to you. She's yours if you want her."

"I probably need my head examined, but yes, I want her. How could I give her up after seeing her?" The puppy licked the tip of Shayla's nose, and Shayla laughed again in response. "Is this how you find homes for all your puppies, Mr. O'Connell?"

"Hey, you do whatever works."

She looked at him again, felt his warm smile all the way down to her toes. "That's dirty pool."

He shrugged even as his grin broadened. "So shoot me."

"Don't tempt me," she retorted.

But shooting him was the last thing she would have wanted to do.

They made a cute picture, the tiny sheltie and the curly-haired woman. He especially liked the way Shayla's dark blue eyes sparkled with pleasure. He'd bet she was the type to stop and smell the roses.

Although he knew he should head back to the ranch, he settled once again onto the steps. "So what're you gonna call her?"

"I don't know." She held the puppy at arm's length and studied her. "What are her parents' names?"

"The bitch is Paradise Belle. Her sire, Lakeside's Shadow Boy, lives up in the Coeur d'Alene area."

Shayla's eyes widened slightly. "This isn't just *any* puppy, is it?"

"What do you mean?"

"I mean those are mighty fancy-sounding names for regular pets." She frowned, her gaze suddenly suspicious. "How much are you selling the rest of the litter for?"

He got up. "The usual," he answered offhandedly, then headed for his truck to retrieve a temporary supply of puppy food and dog necessities. "Feel free to bring her with you tomorrow. No point in her staying here alone all day." He got into the pickup, then held his arm out the window and waved. "See you in the morning."

With that he started the engine and drove away.

Chapter Four

Bleary-eyed from a predominantly sleepless night—thanks to the cries of a puppy newly separated from its mama—Shayla followed the two-mile driveway toward the ranch house, a cloud of dust rising in the compact's wake. Beside her on the car seat, Honey Girl, as the sheltie had been christened, dozed, muzzle on front paws.

"Sure, *you* can sleep," Shayla muttered while stroking the pup's head.

As she drew closer to the house and outbuildings, she caught a glimpse of gray out of the corner of her eye. She turned her head and saw Ian cantering his horse toward a small herd of grazing Herefords. She let up on the gas and allowed the car to coast to a stop so she could watch.

It was a beautiful sight, observing the way horse and rider moved as a single unit rather than separate entities.

She'd attended a few rodeos in her lifetime, so she wasn't totally ignorant of the way cutting horses worked. But this was different. This was the real thing, not some show for a stadium full of greenhorns. She was left almost breathless by the sight.

Ian rode with skill and ease, even when the horse set its front legs, then abruptly changed directions. He held a lariat in his right hand while holding the reins with his left. His black cowboy hat was pulled low on his forehead, shading his eyes from the bright morning sunshine.

"I think I could watch him all day long."

As soon as the words were out of her mouth, she felt the heat of embarrassment rush to her cheeks. That sort of thinking had to be driven straight out of her mind. Murder and mayhem, not romance, should be occupying her thoughts. She was a writer, not a rodeo groupie.

Resolutely she turned her gaze onto the road ahead and pressed on the gas pedal. The car jumped forward, the four-cylinder engine whining its usual tune.

Ian must have heard it, because he rode into the barnyard just a minute or two after she'd arrived at her destination and turned off the engine.

"Morning," he called.

She got out of the car, Honey Girl in her arms.

He reined in his horse, then swung down from the saddle, leaving the reins trailing on the ground as he strode toward her.

"Good morning." Her mouth felt dry as cotton. She moistened her lips with the tip of her tongue.

"How's the pup?"

"Noisy and messy."

He grinned. "Yeah, aren't they though? Did you give her a name yet?"

"Honey Girl."

"Good choice. It fits her."

Whimpering, Honey wriggled, trying to get down. Shayla set her on the ground. For a moment, she watched the puppy scampering through the tulips and daffodils that bordered the porch. But eventually her gaze was drawn back to Ian. He was still looking at her, still smiling.

"I've got a small kennel off the back porch where you can keep her while you're working." He tipped his hat back slightly. "That way you can stop and play with her whenever you like."

Oh, her reckless heart. Thumping away like a bongo player. This was just too incredible for words. And it was unlike her. She wasn't given to lusting after handsome men like Ian—and certainly none had ever given her the time of day.

"Murder and mayhem," she repeated softly to herself. She had to think of Ian O'Connell as nothing more than potential research material. Nothing more than a model for Chet Morrison.

"Something wrong?" Ian asked.

She realized she'd been staring at him for the longest time. Her cheeks flushed hot for the second time in less than fifteen minutes.

"No," she answered. "I was just thinking. About my book," she added quickly. Then she hurried after Honey Girl, glad for a distraction.

Ian shook his head in bemusement as he strode toward the barn a few minutes later. Shayla was a strange one, all right. He couldn't quite get a handle on her. One minute she was all smiles and laughter. The next she was as flustered as a wet hen. One time she'd seem real

sure of herself. The next it seemed she didn't have a lick
of confidence.

And then there was the way she talked to herself. A
hundred years ago, they would've locked her up in an
asylum. Or at least in the attic of the family home.
They'd have thought her loco for certain.

Well, maybe that's how city folk were now days. Living with air pollution from millions of cars probably did
something to their brains. All that traffic and all those
people everywhere you turned would be enough to drive
anyone crazy and have you talking to yourself.

He opened the gate to the kennels to let Bonny and
Coira out. Then he fed and watered them, as well as
Belle and her pups. When that was done, he entered the
barn to saddle a new horse. A glance at his watch told
him he'd better hurry. He was supposed to meet Ty out
by the irrigation ditch in another half an hour.

Dragging his saddle off the saddle tree, he wondered
again why anyone would want to live like people did in
the big cities. If it was him, he'd head for the hills just
as quick as he could. Maybe that's what Shayla had
done. Maybe this was where she'd come running *to*.

No. That wasn't likely. It almost always worked the
other way around.

If he was smart, he'd quit thinking about the little
flatlander and get on with his day. What she did, the
reasons that had brought her here, were her own business
and no concern of his. Best he remember that.

Three hours later, Shayla knelt on the kitchen floor,
scrubbing it for all she was worth. Perspiration beaded
her forehead and dampened her underarms. Straggly
curls fell forward into her face, refugees from her po-

nytail, and she constantly had to push them away with the back of her hand.

She was just about finished when she heard the creak of the rear screen door opening, then closing. She sat back on her heels and glanced over her shoulder. But instead of Ian, as she'd expected, there was another cowboy standing there, this one with golden hair, brown eyes and two-day old stubble on his jaw.

And dirty boots on her clean floor!

"Hey!" she shouted at him. "I just mopped."

He stepped backward, into the small mudroom adjacent to the kitchen. "Sorry, ma'am."

"It's all right," she mumbled, not meaning a word of it.

He removed his hat. "I forgot the boss said he had someone coming in to do the housecleanin'. I'm real sorry 'bout my boots, ma'am."

Ma'am? The word made her feel ancient. She wished he would quit using it.

"We've been irrigatin' all mornin'. Again, I'm right sorry about dirtyin' your floor." He looked it, too. Then he grinned. "My name's Ty. Ty Sheffield. What's yours?"

"Shayla Vincent."

"Pleased to meet you, ma'am."

She couldn't stop herself from laughing softly as she rose to her feet. "Shayla will do quite nicely." If he called her ma'am again, she was going to throw the scrub brush at him.

"You're the one living over at the Erickson place."

"It's *my* place now."

"Well, if you ever need any help, all you gotta do is ask me."

"Thanks."

The screen door creaked again. A moment later, Ian appeared behind Ty. Shayla felt her heart flip in her chest. Like flapjacks on the grill, she thought.

Oh my. Now she was starting to *think* like them.

"Careful, boss." Ty held out an arm to stop Ian from going around him. "She's likely to wallop you if you track mud all over the place. You know how women are about their clean floors."

Shayla supposed a true feminist would be offended by his remarks, but try as she might, she couldn't summon indignation. He'd meant to pay her a compliment, and so she accepted it as such.

"The kitchen hasn't looked this good in years," Ian said in agreement, drawing her gaze to him. "I didn't expect you to get so much done in one morning."

"I come from a big family," she answered, hoping to shake off the spell he seemed to have cast over her. "You learn young how to clean things fast."

"We were coming in for a bite to eat." Before she could reply, Ian added, "We'll use the bootjack first so we don't track up the floor."

Shayla envisioned how she must look, standing there with her messy hair, sweaty shirt and soapy-water-dampened Levi's. So what was new? She always looked dreadful when he was around. It was preordained or something.

"Care to join us for lunch?" he asked as he entered the kitchen in his stocking feet.

She ran a hand over her hair. "Well, I hadn't—"

"No point you driving back to your place. There's plenty to eat here." He headed for the large refrigerator. "You like tuna salad sandwiches? It's all ready except for spreading it on the bread."

"Tuna salad?"

"Bet you thought us cowpokes only ate beef and beans," Ty said as he came to stand beside her.

She nodded. "Yes, I suppose I did."

Ty pointed toward Ian. "The boss here's somewhat of a gourmet cook." He winked at her. "Comes from livin' in this big ol' house all by his lonesome for so many years, I reckon. Nothin' else to do but learn to cook."

She wanted to ask how many years he had been alone. Instead she bent over and lifted the bucket of soapy water. "I'll just get rid of this, then freshen up a bit."

"You'll find whatever you need in that first bathroom at the top of the stairs," Ian told her.

She carried the bucket into the mudroom, dumped its contents into the extradeep sink, then beat a hasty retreat to the second-floor bathroom.

A few minutes after Shayla disappeared, Ty leaned a hip against the counter, watching as Ian prepared a plate full of sandwiches. "She's cute."

"Is she?" Ian replied, then nonchalantly licked some tuna salad from his fingertips.

His young friend chuckled. "As if you haven't noticed."

He ignored that.

"Well, then, I guess that means she's fair game. Always did like tiny gals with curly hair."

Ian shrugged, at the same time pressing his lips together tightly.

"What d'ya know about her?"

"Not much."

"C'mon, Ian. Spill, will you?"

"Okay. Okay," he said impatiently as he snapped the plastic lid onto the container, then shoved it into the leftover-crowded refrigerator. "She's a writer. Came here from Portland to write a novel. A murder mystery, she says. Got a passel of brothers and sisters." He carried the platter of sandwiches to the oak table against the wall opposite the windows. "That's it. That's all I know."

"And no steady boyfriend?"

He felt unreasonably irritable. "I guess not, given she's here alone."

"Couples have been known to keep those long-distance relationships. Silly notion, if you ask me. When you love each other, you stay together."

Ty's words sent Ian's thoughts speeding back in time, back to the day Joanne had packed her suitcase to leave....

"It doesn't mean the marriage is over, Ian." His wife had turned toward him. "I just need...some time away. That's all. Some time to myself. I'll spend a few months at the artists' colony, and then I'll come back."

She was lying—and they both knew it.

"We've been married eight years, Joanne. Don't you think—"

"That's just it!" Her voice rose in frustration. "We've been married eight years and we've never done anything but raise Herefords and quarter horses and collies. We never go anywhere, except down to the café for breakfast and an occasional movie in McCall. I need more than that!"

Ian raked his fingers through his hair. He wanted to tell her they should have been raising kids by now, but he wisely resisted the impulse.

"Jo, you know how hard it is for a rancher to take any real time off."

"Yes, I *do* know. That's the problem." Her words came out like a sigh. Her green eyes were filled with unspeakable sadness, disillusionment, heartache. Then she turned toward the bed and snapped closed her suitcase.

"Jo…" He reached out, placed his hands on her shoulders. "Honey…"

She slipped from beneath his touch. "I want things you don't want," she whispered, "and the same goes for you."

The words cut him like a knife. Because they were true.

He'd known they were drifting apart, known she didn't want the ranch or children, known she might not even want him. He'd known all of that for a long time. He just hadn't wanted to face it.

His wife was unhappy. For that matter, so was he. They fought more often than they made love, and sometimes the words they flung at each other were downright cruel.

But he'd meant his wedding vows, the ones about till death would they part. There'd never been a divorce in the O'Connell family, and he didn't want to be the first. Marriages were supposed to be worked at, to be made to last, no matter what. You hung on, and eventually they got better again.

Joanne and he had been happy once. They'd fallen in love in high school and had married right after graduation. Her family had been in the valley almost as long as the O'Connells. She knew this place and she knew him. Nobody knew him better.

At least that's what he'd believed all these years.

Until now.

"Just let me go, Ian. If you ever loved me, let me go."

Shayla splashed her face with cold water, then used the washcloth to freshen the rest of her. She found a small bottle of musk-scented cologne in the medicine cabinet and sprayed some on her wrists. She was thankful that she'd had the foresight to bring a clean top and a pair of shorts to change into when it got warmer. She quickly donned them before attempting to put her bird's-nest hairdo in order. When she'd done the best she could with what she had, she turned off the light and left the bathroom.

She paused a moment in the hallway, her gaze alighting on an oil painting at the head of the stairs. She knew without looking for the signature that it must have been painted by Ian's late wife. Shayla didn't have to be an art critic to recognize the similarities between this smaller landscape and the much larger one in the great room. Or to recognize the woman's extraordinary talent.

"How long has it been since she died?" she whispered as she reached out to touch the picture frame. "How long has he been alone in this house?"

Years, he had said. But how many years? Enough to put the pain to rest? Or was he still in love with his wife's memory?

She glanced toward the open doorway of his bedroom. She wondered if she would find a photograph of the late Mrs. Ian O'Connell in there. Perhaps on his nightstand or on the fireplace mantel.

Well, she'd know soon enough. She would be tackling the clutter in these upstairs rooms before the end of the week.

And what possible difference could it make to her, one way or the other?

Taking a deep breath, she turned away from the bedroom and walked down the stairs, determined to put a stop to her wayward thoughts. Her determination lasted a good thirty seconds, and then was obliterated by the sound of Ian's hearty laughter coming from the kitchen. Ty was laughing, too, but it was only Ian's that made her pulse race.

She stopped dead still, willing herself to breathe slowly. It would be nothing short of insane if she allowed these reactions to continue. She had to control both her thoughts and her feelings. After all, she'd never been successful in the romance department. Her luck with men was worse than her luck with the lottery. At most, she'd won a few bucks in the latter. She'd come up totally empty in the former.

She swallowed hard, then moved forward cautiously, stopping again when she reached the kitchen doorway. Ian and Ty were already at a large table, a platter of sandwiches and a large pitcher of ice tea in its center. Ian's chair was turned with its back to the wall. He sat in it, slightly slouched, his long legs stretched out in front of him, crossed at the ankles. He held a tall glass of ice tea in one hand, ice cubes clinking against the sides. His black hair still bore the stamp of his cowboy hat. Her fingers itched to smooth it.

Ty noticed her then, and he rose from his chair. "Ma'am," he said with a broad smile. He pulled out the chair next to him. "Sit yourself down."

"Thanks." She allowed herself a quick glance toward Ian, saying, "Sorry it took me so long."

"Wasn't all that long," Ty answered. "And the wait

was worth it, if you don't mind me sayin' so. You look prettier'n a blue jay in a ponderosa pine.''

She hoped she wasn't blushing. She didn't want either of them to guess how seldom she received compliments. Besides, Ty was simply being polite.

''The boss and I were talkin' about the dance over at the Grange Hall next Saturday night. I was hopin' you might go with me.''

She couldn't help herself. She looked toward Ian. Had he thought to ask her? Had Ty beat him to it?

''You ought to go, Shayla.'' Ian held out the platter of sandwiches. ''You'd meet plenty of your neighbors. Even more than you did on Sunday. Folks always have a good time at the Grange dances. Chad Friday plays a mean fiddle, and Pastor Barnett on the drums is something nobody should miss. I never do if I can help it.''

His words told her he didn't mind that Ty had asked her to the dance, that he didn't care if she went with him. And the knowledge caused sharp disappointment to pierce through her.

''What d'ya say?'' Ty persisted. ''Will you go with me, Shayla?''

''Yes,'' she answered softly, turning toward the blond-haired cowboy. ''I would like to go. Thank you for asking me.''

Since Ian had been a small boy, he'd liked sitting on the wide, wraparound porch on summer evenings, watching as sunset settled over the earth, the sinking sun gilding the grasslands in shades of gold and orange before giving over to the pewter tones of nightfall. This hour of the day, more often than not, brought with it a breeze to sway the tall pines that towered above the house, a hundred feet and more, rolling them in huge arcs, enough to make a man dizzy if he stared upward for too long.

It was a silent part of Ian's day. His year-round ranch hands, Ty Sheffield and Mick Janssen, had returned to their own homes to be with their own families. The livestock had been fed and watered, and those animals that required it were in the stalls in the barn. Dinner was over, the dishes washed and put away.

Now it was just him and his dogs, the sunset and the evening breeze. Bonny lay beside his wooden rocking chair. Coira sat closer to him, her muzzle resting on his thigh. Belle was down on the lawn with her remaining three pups.

Ian wondered if Shayla would get more sleep tonight or if Honey Girl would continue to cry for her lost mama. Dollars to doughnuts, she'd take that puppy into her bed before the week was out. She seemed the sort.

He turned his eyes to the west, toward the Erickson cabin. Or should he call it the Vincent cabin now?

Nothing ever happens here! Joanne's complaint rang in his ears, as strong now as it had been when she'd first said it. *We might as well be living in a cave. I'm tired of being snowbound in the winter. I want to do something! I want to go somewhere!*

He'd be wise to go on thinking of that place as the Erickson cabin, because he'd bet good money Shayla Vincent wouldn't last through Christmas. When the heavy snows came and the temperature plummeted to below zero and the power lines snapped or the phones went dead, she'd pack her clothes and computer into that noisy little car of hers and hightail it back to Portland.

"Best place for her, too. Flatlanders ought to stay where they belong."

Coira slapped a paw onto his thigh, drawing his gaze. The dog was watching him with big, sad eyes.

"She won't last," he told the collie. "She seems to be real nice, and I hope she has a good time at the dance with Ty. But I also hope that boy doesn't get his tail in a knot over her, 'cause she won't be staying." He stroked the dog's head. "And you and I both know that, don't we, girl?"

And yet, even as he spoke, there was a part of him, deep in a corner of his heart, that wished he'd asked her to the dance before Ty, because...

Because what if she *did* last through Christmas?

Chapter Five

Shayla didn't see much of Ian over the next three days. Although he greeted her warmly enough when she arrived each morning he would then immediately head for the barn, saddle up one of his horses and ride off, not to be seen again for the remainder of the day.

Ty Sheffield was another story altogether. The young cowboy found a reason at least once each day to return to the ranch house, and when he did, he always took a few minutes to visit with Shayla. She discovered she enjoyed his company. Besides being charming and well mannered, he had a fun sense of humor and an easygoing nature. Like her, he was the eldest child of a large family, giving them an immediate connection and understanding. It wasn't long before she felt as if she knew him as well as she knew one of her own brothers.

She recognized when she was being given the rush, even when it was done cowboy-style. She was actually a little flattered by it, especially after learning she was six years his senior. After all, being pursued wasn't a common occurrence in her life. She even wished she could return his apparent affection.

But when she went home each afternoon and sat staring at the blinking cursor on her computer screen, it wasn't Ty she thought about. It was Ian's image that drifted through her mind, with his inky black hair and coffee-colored eyes....

On Friday morning at the end of that first week, Shayla and Honey were greeted by the two black-and-white border collies as they drove up to the ranch house. Ian stood on the porch, drinking coffee from a large mug, dressed in his usual boots, jeans, Western shirt and black Stetson.

"Morning," he called to her as she climbed out of her car.

"Good morning."

"Better close your windows. We're in for some thundershowers later on."

She glanced upward. Except for a smattering of pristine white clouds on the horizon, all she saw was blue. "Rain?" She frowned. "Doesn't look like it to me."

"That can change quick enough."

"You sound awfully sure of yourself." She set Honey on the ground and watched her scamper after the older dogs.

"Yup."

She walked toward the house while keeping an eye on the puppy. "Do you have a bad knee that warns you when the weather's about to change?"

"Nope. Something even better than that. I've got a satellite dish and The Weather Channel."

She stopped at the base of the steps and looked up at

him. He was wearing a teasing grin that caused her heart to begin that wretched erratic thumping.

"How's your oven working?" he asked, abruptly changing the subject.

"Fine. No more trouble since you put in the new element."

"Good."

There wasn't any doubt about it. He was the most devastatingly handsome man she'd ever laid eyes on, and she was much too attracted to him for her own good.

"Come on in. We can talk over a cup of coffee before we both get to work."

She nodded, not certain what this change in routine meant.

She glanced behind her, then clucked her tongue at Honey who came running toward her in response, tripping over her own paws and somersaulting to a halt a few feet away from her mistress. Shayla laughed as she bent to pick up the puppy.

"Clumsy, aren't you?" she said softly.

And she felt just as clumsy a moment later as she followed Ian into the house, her heart tripping over itself. She was ridiculously pleased that he was going to spend a few minutes with her this morning.

As soon as they were both seated at the kitchen table, large mugs of strong coffee in front of them, Ian said, "I wanted to tell you what a great job you've been doing. My mom couldn't have made it look better, and she's a real stickler for details."

"Thanks."

"Are you an equally good secretary?" He tipped his chair back on its hind legs until the high back touched the wall behind him.

"I like to think so. I enjoy it more than cleaning house. That's for sure."

He grinned. "Tell me how you got started."

"Nothing special. I thought it would be just a summer job. I answered an ad right after graduation from high school. I started at minimum wage since I had no decipherable skills to begin with. I ended up working for the company for the next twelve years. I took night classes in computers and bookkeeping and such. Those classes helped earn me a few promotions."

"So why'd you leave?"

"I wouldn't have if things had continued on the same. But the business folded, and I was out of a job. It was very sudden. Nobody saw it coming, except the CEO and a few higher-up executives, and they never let on to the rest of us."

She sipped her coffee, thinking back over the events of this past spring.

"My boss gave me a glowing letter of recommendation, and my folks invited me to live at home again while I hunted for a new job." She met his gaze. "But then I realized this was my chance to do what I've been wanting to do for years. I knew the chance might not come again. I had to grab it or lose it forever." Softly she added, "My parents think I'm crazy."

"It takes a lot of guts to do what you did."

"Do you think so?"

"Yes." He stared into space, a far-off look in his eyes, as if he could see something she couldn't. "Yes, I do think so."

She almost reached out to touch him, to comfort him somehow.

"Following a dream always takes courage," he said, his voice sounding as far away as his gaze. "Because it changes everything. Not just for yourself but for those who love you. You can't ever go back to the way things were before.''

He suddenly let his chair rock forward. He put down his mug, then rose to his feet.

"I'd better get busy. We'll have a short working day with those storms blowing in."

And with that, he strode from the kitchen, leaving Shayla wondering what it was she'd seen in his eyes and heard in his voice.

Ian had been thinking a lot about Joanne in the last week. More than he'd thought about her in years. And he couldn't say he cared much for it. He'd thought that was all behind him, that he'd laid it to rest long ago.

Apparently he'd been wrong.

As Blue picked the way up a shale-covered trail, Ian remembered again those last years of his marriage, remembered the way it had felt, seeing his wife changing before his eyes. She had discovered oil painting quite by accident, and once she'd begun, nothing else had been as important to her.

Not even him.

She'd turned one of the upstairs bedrooms into her studio—a bedroom that he'd always thought would be the nursery. She'd spent hours poring over books about the great masters, about different painting techniques. That first summer, she'd driven down to Boise twice each week to take lessons from some teacher who was supposed to be one of the best instructors in the Northwest. Everybody had said Joanne possessed an extraordinary talent that should be developed.

But Ian had wanted a wife who was involved in the everyday workings of a thriving cattle ranch. He'd wanted children—a houseful of them—not more oil paintings on his walls.

At the top of the ridge, he stopped his horse and dismounted. Then he stood there, staring down at the crystal-clear mountain lake below.

Joanne had loved him once, but she'd needed something he hadn't been able to give her. It wasn't pleasant, admitting the part he'd played in the disintegration of his marriage. Their love had died by inches; it had been painful, watching it deteriorate and crumble before his eyes. Joanne had had a dream to follow, and she'd had the courage to follow it. But he'd tried to stop her. He'd tried to make her want only what he wanted. He'd been immature, stubborn, selfish.

Maybe if he hadn't been all those things, Joanne would be alive today. Maybe they would still be married. Maybe they would have the children he'd always wanted. And maybe his childhood sweetheart would be famous, her paintings hanging in galleries from New York City to Los Angeles.

Only God knew what might have been if she hadn't died while running away...from him.

"I'm sorry, Jo. I should've understood. I should've tried harder," he murmured.

Shayla Vincent also had a dream to pursue. And although she hadn't said it in so many words, he suspected nobody close to her understood that dream or how important it was. He hoped they wouldn't try to take it away from her.

For some crazy, inexplicable reason, he was determined to help make sure they didn't.

Clasping a caddy full of cleaning products, rags and brushes, Shayla opened the door to the first bedroom on the second floor. But what she discovered there was an artist's studio instead of a bedroom.

His *wife's* studio.

There was a faint odor of oil paint and turpentine in the closed room. A strangely disturbing odor. It made Shayla feel like an intruder.

Which was ridiculous. She wasn't an intruder. She was *supposed* to be there.

She set the caddy on a small folding table, then crossed the room. She turned the latches and lifted each of the three windows, letting in a rush of fresh air. Afterward she turned to survey her surroundings.

A thick layer of dust covered all the surfaces, but the room wasn't as cluttered as the rest of the house. There was a bookcase containing how-to-paint books, books on the history of art and others whose contents couldn't be easily discerned by their titles alone. Art magazines were neatly stored in plastic magazine racks in one corner. Blank canvases were stacked against the far wall. An empty easel stood in the center of the room, turned toward the windows, she supposed for the best light. An organizer cart on casters had been placed near the easel. She suspected the five drawers of the cart were filled with paintbrushes, tubes of oil paint and other supplies. She wondered how long it had been since any of them had been used.

Turning around, she spied a grouping of three portraits on the same wall as the door: portraits of Ian O'Connell.

She walked toward them, feeling the quickening of her heart as she did so. The largest of the three paintings showed the cowboy on horseback. Pine-covered mountains served as a backdrop, and several Hereford cattle grazed nearby. Dressed in his usual Western attire, he sat on the horse with ease, a half smile lifting one corner of his mouth. His eyes were shaded by the brim of his hat, and yet she felt as if he were staring—and smiling—right at her.

She shifted her gaze to the second painting. This one showed Ian sitting in the tall grass, his head bare, hat on the ground beside him. He was surrounded by several border collies, although their markings were different from either Bonny or Coira. He was laughing as one of the dogs licked his chin, his head thrown back, his face bathed in sunshine. She could almost hear his laughter, it seemed so real.

The third painting was much darker than the other two, in both mood and colors. The setting was nightfall, the color scheme predominately shades of blue, gray and black. Ian was standing at a corral fence, one boot resting on the lower rail, his arms crossed on the top one. He was staring into the distance; his expression was one of longing and great loss.

She felt an unreasonable urge to weep for him.

"She was very good, wasn't she?"

Shayla whirled toward the doorway.

Ian stood there, hat in hand. "Better than I wanted her to be."

It seemed an odd thing to say.

"She would've gone far, probably been famous." He stepped into the room.

"How long has she been…gone?"

"Ten years."

"Ten?"

"Long time, isn't it? I know I should've gotten rid of all this. It's just going to waste. But I…" He shrugged, then came to stand beside her, his gaze now on the portraits. "She did those two—" he motioned toward the one with him on horseback and the one with the dogs

"—that first year after she took art lessons in Boise." He pointed to the darker one. "This one was the last she painted before she died."

"How…" She closed her mouth before the rest of the question could come out.

But he understood. "How did she die? Car accident. She was driving south of here on the highway. She was on her way to stay at an artist's colony. A logging truck overturned right in front of her. The logs broke loose and rolled over the top of her car, crushing it. She was killed instantly." He paused a moment, then said, "She wasn't quite twenty-six."

"How tragic."

"Joanne never got the chance to do what she wanted before she died." He looked at her. "Don't let anything or anyone stop you, Shayla. You may not get another chance to write that book of yours."

"That's why I came here."

He slapped his Stetson onto his head. "I'm taking the truck into town to order the supplies we'll need to repair your roof. I ought to be back in an hour or so." He strode out of the studio without another word.

For a moment, Shayla stared after him. Then she turned toward the paintings again, her gaze drawn to that third, darker portrait.

She had a feeling the canvas told a lot more about him than she understood as yet.

The usual group of men were hanging around the hardware store that afternoon. Ian nodded to them before walking to the counter.

"How's it going, Ed?" he said to the owner.

Ed Clark was an obese man in his early sixties with three chins and a head as bald as a bowling ball. Years ago, liquored up on a cold Saturday night, he'd put gasoline into his stove to help the wood catch fire. He was lucky all he'd lost in the resulting explosion were his eyebrows. He hadn't tasted a drop of whiskey since— nor had his eyebrows grown back, which accounted for the surprised expression he always seemed to wear.

"You back so soon, O'Connell? That gal's oven didn't go out again, did it?"

"No. She says it's working fine. It's roofing supplies I'm after this time."

"Sure thing. Gonna be fixing your roof this summer, huh?"

There was no point in trying to keep one's business to oneself in a town this size. Ian had learned that long ago. It was easier just to answer folks' questions from the get-go. Caused a man less grief in the long run.

"Not mine," he answered Ed. "I'm making repairs to Miss Vincent's roof. On the old Erickson cabin. We're working an exchange. She's giving my house a good scouring, and I'm going to make a few repairs to hers."

"Cedar shake, isn't it? Her roof."

"Yes."

"Leaking when it rains?"

"Yes."

"Well, let's see what we can do about that."

For the next hour, the two men talked roofing supplies and techniques. Ed might be a man too large to move quickly and too heavy to climb a tall ladder, but he had a sharp mind and he knew about construction, lumber and hardware. He was a virtual font of information.

By the time the order was written up and they'd exchanged a bit of town gossip, Ian noticed the store was growing dark. He turned toward the storefront windows, only to discover roiling black clouds had arrived while he'd been inside.

"I'd better get a move on," he said. "Don't like the looks of that sky."

"Sure thing. I'll have all these items you ordered by Monday."

"Thanks." He said his farewells to the other men in the hardware store, then hurried out to his pickup.

He was just driving out of town when the first bolt of lightning flashed toward the ground, followed quickly by a deafening crash of thunder. It was probably too early in the season for any real danger of forest or grass fires. But all the same, he preferred to be at home and watchful when a storm like this one blew into the valley. Better safe than sorry.

He pressed down on the gas pedal.

When what sounded like an explosion right above her head shook the big house to its foundations, Shayla let out a shriek, then rushed to the nearby window to look outside.

She'd never seen such an ugly, angry sky before. Clouds as black as night swept over the mountain peaks, churning like a storm-tossed sea. A fork of lightning suddenly lit up the valley, connecting sky to earth. The hair on the back of her neck stood on end as a loud crack assaulted her ears.

"Honey Girl!" she cried, remembering the puppy out in the kennel.

She raced from the guest room, down the stairs, through the kitchen and out the back door. The sheltie was cowering in a corner, whimpering in fear.

"It's okay, girl," she said as she opened the gate.

"It's okay." She picked up the quivering puppy. "Oh, you poor thing. You poor little thing."

Another flash of lightning. Another crack of thunder. Shayla squealed again, then hightailed it back into the house, feeling as frightened as the young dog in her arms.

She hated thunderstorms. Always had.

She took shelter in an overstuffed chair in the great room, as far from the window as she could get. She cuddled Honey Girl close to her chest, pressed her face against the puppy's soft coat and closed her eyes, dreading the next crash that would shake the house.

And it did.

Again and again and again.

To Shayla, it seemed like the coming of Armageddon. The end of the world could be no more terrifying than this. Not to her anyway.

The wind began to howl, stirring up dust and pebbles from the barnyard, pelting the sides of the house.

Rat-a-tat-tat.

Rat-a-tat-tat.

It sounded like a machine gun. Even knowing what it was didn't help. It was still a frightening sound, especially with her eyes squeezed shut.

That's how Ian found her.

"Hey, what's this?" he asked gently. "Afraid of a bit of lightning?"

She felt his arms go around her, and she willingly allowed it. He sat beside her, pulling her onto his lap. He was big and strong and safe, and she could hide her face against his broad chest instead of against the small, quivering puppy. His large, callused hand stroked her hair with surprising gentleness. He murmured comforting words while the storm raged overhead, and little by little, her terror lessened.

Except for the soft patter of raindrops upon the porch roof and the faint ticking of the clock on the mantel, all was quiet. The storm had moved across the valley and beyond the eastern mountains, the thunder fading until it was silenced altogether. And yet Ian continued to hold her, his arms warm around her, his heartbeat melding with her own.

She felt her cheeks grow warm with embarrassment. Or maybe it was the flush of pleasure. Regardless, she straightened, drew away, slid from his lap and stood. She didn't want to look at him, but she knew she must.

"I...I'm sorry," she said.

He stood, too. "No reason to be sorry." His gaze was compassionate, understanding.

"You must think me a terrible baby." She brushed the tearstains from her cheeks.

"We've all got our private demons."

She had the insane desire to return to the warmth of his embrace. Instead she took a step backward. "I've always been terrified by lightning and thunder. I don't know why."

"How about a cup of something hot to soothe the nerves?" He held out his hand, as if to take her arm.

She nodded in acquiescence. "I'll put Honey in the kennel." Then she led the way to the kitchen, thinking it better if she didn't allow him to touch her again.

Chapter Six

The dawn the next morning was spectacular, as was often the case after a storm. Lacy clouds were tinged with pinks and lavenders, the sky itself a powdery blue. The fresh fragrance of rain-washed earth and pines lingered in the air. A doe and her fawn grazed in a clearing on the mountainside while a hawk circled overhead in search of unsuspecting prey.

Ian observed it all from horseback, having arisen early after a relatively sleepless night.

He'd been thinking about Shayla.

He hadn't been conscious of it then, but it had felt mighty good, holding her on his lap, his arms keeping her close against him. She had seemed so fragile, so wonderfully feminine. Flowers. She'd smelled of wildflowers. And there had been the rapid beating of her heart so close to his own. He wasn't sure if he'd actually heard it at the time, but he seemed able to hear it now.

He looked north. Her cabin was obscured by ponderosa and lodgepole pines, aspens and tamaracks. But he knew its precise location and how it would look with lemony sunlight kissing the peak of the roof just about now.

Had she slept well? Better than him, he hoped.

She'd made it clear that she hadn't been comfortable around him once her fear was gone. She'd decided to cut her day short, staying only long enough to have a cup of tea—and doing that only out of politeness. Then she'd put away her cleaning supplies and left.

Maybe there *was* some fella back in Portland. But if so, why had she agreed to go to the dance tonight with Ty? No, it was only Ian whom she felt uncomfortable around. And that knowledge bothered him.

"I've been too long without a woman," he muttered.

That was the only explanation for him thinking about her this way. Shayla wasn't his type. He liked tall, slender gals with long, straight hair. He liked women in Levi's, boots and cowboy hats, women who could talk horses and cattle as easily as they could talk kids and cooking, women who knew a half-diamond hitch from a granny knot.

That sure as heck didn't describe Shayla Vincent. She wouldn't know a granny knot from a hole in the ground. He'd bet his best heifer on it.

Yet, the truth was, he'd spent the better part of the last week with that cute little flatlander on his mind— kinky brown curls, dark blue eyes and all. She had grit, that one. Grit, determination and courage. He had to admire that quality in anyone, man or woman.

But admiration wasn't what he'd been feeling yesterday when he'd held her in his arms. No, what he'd felt then was the desire to go right on holding her. And once her terror of the storm had passed, what he'd wanted to do was kiss her.

"Well, I'll be doggoned."

He'd be plumb loco if he went and did anything like that. Once before he'd tied his future to an artistic-minded woman who hadn't wanted the same things he did. He wasn't going to knowingly let that happen to him a second time.

Not if he could help it, he wouldn't.

"I never should have agreed to go," Shayla said as she glared at her reflection in the mirror.

She hadn't a clue what she should wear to a Grange dance. She didn't even know what a Grange was, for pity sake. Regardless, she certainly shouldn't have chosen this dress from the clothes in her closet. It made her look short and frumpy.

Of course, she *was* short and frumpy. There'd never been a time when those adjectives hadn't described her.

A glance at her wristwatch told her it was too late to change into something else. Ty was due any moment. In fact, there was the sound of a vehicle pulling into her drive right now.

Releasing a sigh of frustration, she grabbed her purse and a sweater and headed for the door, opening it just as Ty reached the deck.

He had traded his faded work denims for a pair of slim-cut black jeans. His snakeskin boots, peeking from beneath his pant legs, had been polished to a high sheen. His Western shirt was similar to the ones he'd worn all week, but this one was newer, its colors—white, red and black—still bright. And he was obviously wearing a "dress Stetson," a hat kept for Sundays and other special occasions.

Pure cowboy, she thought as she smiled at him.

"Evenin', ma'am."

She wrinkled her nose. "I thought we'd agreed to forego that ma'am stuff. You make me feel old."

"Right you are. Evenin', Shayla."

She stepped onto the deck, closing the door behind her. Ty immediately came forward, took the sweater from her hand and draped it over her shoulders.

"You look prettier'n a heifer in clover."

Looking up at him, she asked, "Do you always talk like that?"

"Like what?"

"Never mind." She laughed softly.

"Yes, ma'am."

She jabbed him in the ribs with her elbow, then took hold of his proffered arm and allowed him to escort her down the steps and out to his Jeep.

"I asked Ian to ride with us," he said as he opened the passenger door, "but he said he'd take his own truck."

Her heart skipped a beat. "Who is he bringing with him?"

"You mean as a date?" He laughed. "Nobody. He hasn't had a girlfriend for quite a spell. Not that there aren't some who'd give their eye teeth for a chance with him. But Ian's been feeling a bit wary ever since Sally Pruitt turned out to be a gold digger."

"How long ago was that?"

"Oh, I don't know. A year maybe. People are still talkin' about it like it was yesterday. Lucky for Ian, she moved up to Spokane not long after it ended. Had to make it easier for him, her being gone." He closed the door, then strode around to the driver's side, got in and started the engine.

"Was he in love with her?"

"Naw. Don't think so. I think he's still a bit gun-shy." He gave her a quick glance as he put the car in gear. "You buckled up?"

"Yes."

"Then let's get a move on. I'm lookin' forward to that first dance with you."

They were silent as the Jeep bumped and bounced its way down the dusty road toward the highway.

Shayla couldn't help looking out the window toward the big house at Paradise Ranch, wondering if Ian was there or if he'd left for the Grange Hall already. Wondering if she would get to dance with him and feel his arms around her once again.

Ian had been watching the entrance for fifteen minutes. He'd managed to carry on a reasonably intelligent conversation with Ed Clark and the Barnetts without looking too distracted. At least he thought he'd carried it off.

He felt a jolt of relief when Shayla finally walked through the door with Ty. He was glad to see they'd arrived safely. Ty's twenty-year-old Jeep wasn't the most reliable vehicle.

Or maybe it wasn't relief he felt when he saw them together. Maybe it was something more akin to jealousy.

"Look, Roger," Geneve Barnett said to her husband. "There's Miss Vincent. Thank goodness someone invited her. It was thoughtless of me not to do so on Sunday. We must go welcome her."

I should have asked her to come with me, Ian thought as he followed the Barnetts with his gaze. *Why didn't I? Why'd I let Ty beat me to it?*

He turned toward Ed. "Think I'll get me something

cool to drink,'' he said, then walked toward the back of the hall, far away from the front door, Shayla and Ty.

For the next half hour, he succeeded in keeping his mind off the couple by involving himself in a conversation with several friends and neighbors, talking about the upcoming school board election. It moved from that topic to the price of beef, and from there it drifted to yesterday's storm.

The storm.

Lightning and thunder.

Shayla, frightened and teary-eyed, cowering in a chair in the great room.

Shayla, nestled in his arms, feeling like she'd always belonged there.

He turned toward the dance floor. Couples were moving quickly in time to a lively tune played by Chad Friday on the fiddle, Walt North on the steel guitar and Pastor Barnett on the drums. It didn't take Ian long to find Shayla in that pretty pink-flowered outfit she was wearing. The hem of the dress whispered around her ankles, then flared out as her partner spun her around.

She was looking up at Ty and laughing as she tried to follow his fancy footwork. Ian would bet good money that she'd never tried to country swing before. She was struggling a bit, but all in all, she wasn't doing too badly.

As the song ended, he said, ''Excuse me,'' to those around him, then walked toward the dance floor, not allowing himself to think about what he was doing. When he arrived at the place where Ty and Shayla were standing, he said, ''You don't mind if I take a turn with Shayla, do you, Ty?''

The young cowboy waved him forward. ''Be my guest. Just remember, she came with me.''

Ian nodded, but his gaze was on Shayla. She wasn't

smiling. He wondered if *she* minded. Maybe he'd asked the wrong person for permission.

The music started. A popular George Strait melody. A slow dance. He hadn't expected that, but he wasn't sorry. How could he be?

He held out his arms in invitation. She slipped her right hand into his left, then stepped close to him. His free hand alighted on the small of her back, just as natural as you please.

"You look very pretty in that dress."

She glanced upward, amusement pulling at the corners of her mouth. "Prettier than a heifer in clover?"

"I guess Ty beat me to the compliment." He raised an eyebrow in question.

"Yes, he did."

"Figures."

They moved together as if they'd done this before. She wasn't struggling to keep up with him as she had with the country swing. Instinctively he drew her closer. She turned her head so that her right cheek rested against his chest. Her hair smelled like wildflowers again; he supposed it was the shampoo she used. He liked it. It suited her.

The song was over too quickly. For a heartbeat after the music stopped, he continued to hold her, continued to move as if it still played. Then, reluctantly, he stopped and stepped back, releasing her from his embrace.

Their gazes met. Hers seemed to reveal emotions as mixed and confused as his own.

She opened her mouth as if to say something. But before she could speak, Ty appeared to reclaim his date. Ian had no choice but to smile, thank her for the dance and walk away.

Walking away was the absolute *last* thing he wanted to do.

Shayla was having a wonderful time. Everyone she'd met had made her feel welcome, as if she were truly a part of the community. Between dances, with Ty standing at her side, she answered questions about herself, her hometown, her writing.

"Portland, huh?" This from Walt North, a grizzled cowboy in his early fifties. "I worked there one year. Long time ago. Rains too much. Damp gets in your bones and never goes away." He shook his head, the action clearly saying, Can't imagine why anyone would want to live there.

"Who's your favorite writer?" Nat Briscoe, next year's Rainbow High senior class president, asked quickly before Walt could start talking again.

"Oh, I have lots of favorites. I'd have to give it some thought before I could name only one." She took a sip of red fruit punch from the tall plastic tumbler in her hand. After a moment, she said, "Mary Higgins Clark was the first writer to make me think I'd like to do it myself. So maybe I would choose her."

"You ever come visit Lauretta when you were a youngster?" asked Hydrangea Zimmerman, a woman in her early seventies with sun-leathered skin and watery blue eyes.

"Yes, I did."

"Well, girl, I think I met you back then. Frecklefaced, with your nose peeling from a sunburn. Just kneehigh to a grasshopper, you were." She chuckled. "Not much different from what you are now."

"That was me."

The wizened old woman, a good two inches shorter

than Shayla, leaned forward and, in a conspiratorial whisper, added, "Don't envy them tall folk. They're always hitting their heads on one thing or another."

"I'll remember that."

"Is this your first book you're working on?" Geneve Barnett inquired.

"Yes. But I've wanted to try my hand at it for many years. Ever since I was in school."

And so the evening went. Only one thing kept it from being perfect...and that was the absence of Ian.

She hadn't seen him since they'd danced together two hours before.

But Ian could see her.

From the darkened balcony at the north end of the Grange Hall, he watched as she mingled, talked, laughed. That lilting laughter that made him smile whenever he heard it. And it wasn't only a smile it brought him. It also lightened his heart, made his insides feel airy, weightless as a cloud.

So that was the way it was going to be, he thought as he stared down from his lofty sanctuary. He wasn't going to listen to his own good sense. He wasn't going to heed the voice of wisdom that told him he would be better off pursuing someone else.

Anybody else.

No, he was going to obey the urging of his heart instead. Maybe it wouldn't lead anywhere. Then again, maybe it would. He might as well find out, one way or the other. No point wasting time wondering.

"Sorry, Ty," he whispered, "but I'm not honoring any claims you might've made on our little mystery writer. All's fair from this point on."

He was up and out of his folding chair the instant he

saw Chad, Walt and Roger walking toward the stage at the opposite end of the hall. He took the narrow staircase three steps at a time. He'd nearly reached Shayla by the time the trio was warming up to begin their last set.

Ty saw his approach. Something in his eyes told Ian he'd guessed what was coming, and he wasn't happy about it.

Too bad.

"Shayla?"

She turned. He caught the glimmer of surprise that flashed in her eyes. And then she smiled at him, the look warm and inviting.

"Can you spare me another turn around the dance floor?"

"Yes." She nodded. "You don't mind, do you, Ty?"

Her date lied through his teeth. "No, I don't mind."

Luck was with Ian. The trio was playing another slow dance. He had another excuse to hold her in his arms.

"You're having a good time?" he asked in a low voice.

"Yes." There was a dreamy look in her eyes as she gazed upward.

"I'm glad."

"And you?"

Dang, if he wouldn't like to kiss her.

"Are you having a good time, too?"

I am now, he thought. But he couldn't say it aloud, so he simply nodded before drawing her closer.

Ian was no stranger to desire, and there was no denying he'd like to do more than simply dance with Shayla. But there was something even stronger going on inside him as he held her close. Something as yet indefinable. But then, he was no wordsmith. That was Shayla's department. He figured he'd just be content to feel whatever it was and not worry about putting a name on it. At least for now.

He danced with her twice more before the band packed up their instruments and folks started home for the night. And as much as he wished he had the privilege of driving Shayla back to her place, he had to settle for getting into his pickup alone.

All the way to Paradise, he hummed softly to himself. But it wasn't until he pulled into the barnyard, cut the engine and turned off the headlights that he recognized the song running through his head. It was the last one they'd danced to. The lyrics included something about taking a chance on love.

He remained in the cab as he silently repeated those words: *Taking a chance on love.*

For a long time now he'd wanted to find the right woman, get married, start a family, but it wasn't until this moment that he realized he hadn't once thought about falling in love again.

He'd loved Joanne with everything in him.

Then he'd let love die.

And then he'd let Joanne die—or so it had seemed to him.

Could he connect with a woman again? Could that person be Shayla? And if he *did* fall for her, would he live to regret it?

He didn't know, but it was dang sure time to find out.

"Thank you, Ty. It was a lovely evening."

"For me, too. Maybe we can do it again sometime."

"Maybe."

She avoided him trying to kiss her on the mouth by placing a hand on his shoulder, then quickly rising on tiptoe to lightly brush his cheek with her lips.

"Good night," she said, then opened the door and slipped inside.

With the door closed again, she sank against it and sighed. She felt like spinning around the room like a ballerina.

You're having a good time?

She closed her eyes, imagining herself in Ian's arms once more.

You look very pretty in that dress.

Funny, how so few words could change one's perspective. Only a few hours ago she'd thought she looked frumpy in it. Now she felt pretty. Pretty because Ian had said she was.

"You're thirty years old," she reminded herself aloud. "Not sixteen."

It didn't make a bit of difference. She *felt* sixteen. All giddy and capricious.

Half walking, half floating, she crossed the living room and entered her bedroom. The moment she flicked on the light, Honey Girl whimpered an excited greeting and scratched at the door of her crate.

"Ready to go outside, little one?"

Shayla opened the door to release the puppy. Honey Girl ran circles around her legs.

"Let's get you outside before you have an accident." She patted her thigh. "Come on, Honey. Outside."

A full moon floated above the mountains in the east, seemingly perched on their craggy peaks, bathing the valley in a blanket of white. The light undulated atop the field grasses, rising and swelling with the whims of the midnight breeze.

In the city, she wouldn't have dared wander outside alone at this time of night. Here, she felt safe doing so.

Here, everything was different.

Fresher. Freer. More alive.

She and Honey strolled down the driveway. When the puppy stopped to piddle, Shayla praised her with great enthusiasm, then they continued their walk, not stopping again until they reached the road.

You look very pretty in that dress.

A quiver of pleasure ran up her spine, so real was the memory of his voice in her mind.

She hadn't returned the compliment, hadn't told him how wonderful he looked. Like Ty, Ian's attire had been a newer, more vividly colored version of the clothes he wore every day. And yet, as handsome as her date had looked, he hadn't made her pulse race the way the sight of Ian had done.

The way the memory of him still did.

Oh my.

She'd always thought summer romances were for teenagers, and she believed a summer romance was the most that could happen between them. Even Ian had told her not to let anything or anyone get in the way of her dream.

Reality came crashing down around her.

He was right. She couldn't let anything get in her way.

Ruthlessly she reined in her emotions. She would not go all soft in the head over that cowboy, no matter how handsome he was, no matter how much he seemed to like her. It would never work anyway. They both knew it.

"Come on, Honey." She turned toward the cabin, at the same time turning her back on Paradise Ranch…and Ian. "Let's go in. There's no reason for us to stay out here any longer."

Chapter Seven

*C*het eyed the dark-haired woman behind the lunch counter. Her name was True, but the whole town knew that wasn't a description of her personality. True Barry could spin a lie faster than anybody in the county and usually did.

The tall brunette had legs up to there, and a body that screamed, Take me, I'm yours. *She was movie-star pretty, too.*

Made a guy wonder what had brought her to this re-mote valley in central Idaho. Was she on the run? Hid-ing out? Or had she come here because the male-female ratio in these parts ran in her favor?

Not that she needed that advantage. There were plenty of men in Eden Valley interested in scoring with True. Chet wasn't one of them. It would be a cold day in you-know-where before he took her up on the nonverbal in-vitation she was issuing to him now. He wouldn't even

*be in the diner, enduring her come-hither stare, except
True knew something about Neal's death. Chet meant to
find out what it was.*

*"What can I get for you, cowboy?" she asked in that
sultry, seductive voice of hers.*

*Okay, so maybe he wasn't entirely immune to her con-
siderable charms.*

*She set the coffeepot on the counter near his plate,
then leaned toward him. So close, he could see the tiny
gold flecks in her eyes. Hazel eyes framed with long
lashes. And if he shifted the direction of his gaze, he
knew he would have an incredible view of her generous
cleavage, too.*

*"You look troubled, cowboy," she said, loud enough
for everyone in the diner to hear. "Maybe I can help
somehow." Then she lowered her voice to a nearly inaudible whisper. "Meet me behind the diner in ten
minutes."*

*"Not interested," he managed to say, despite what his
body was screaming at him.*

"It's about Neal, you idiot. Be there."

*Flashing him another of her sexy smiles, she straight-
ened and walked off to pour coffee for some other cus-
tomer, leaving Chet to wonder what he was going to find
behind the diner.*

The cabin door was open. As Ian approached the deck,
he heard music coming from inside. George Strait was
singing that same tune from last night. The one Ian and
Shayla had danced to.

He couldn't help smiling as he realized the melody
had been haunting her, too. Enough that she'd put it on
the stereo.

Ian climbed the steps, careful not to make any sound.

At the screen door, he stopped and looked in. Shayla was sitting in front of her computer, her back toward the door, her fingers tapping away on the keyboard. *Clickity-clickity-clickity.* She was a fast typist.

He'd seen her in church this morning, but she'd arrived before him and was already seated with the Sheffield family—Ty, his parents and the rest of their children. The most Ian had been able to do was give Shayla a quick greeting. To try to do more would have been awkward.

And so here he was, coming to her place on this Sunday afternoon. Last week he'd brought her a puppy. Today he'd brought a saddle horse.

He rapped on the door. She typed a few more words, probably finishing an idea, then swiveled her chair. A look of surprise—or was it something else?—filled her eyes an instant before she rose to her feet.

"Ian."

"Sorry for interrupting your work." Maybe he shouldn't have come.

"It's all right." She crossed the room. "I was ready for a break anyway. I've been at it ever since I got home from church." She opened the screen door. "Would you like a glass of ice tea or something?"

"Actually, I came over to see if you'd like to go for a ride." He motioned behind him. "I brought a horse for you to use. Just in case."

"A horse?" She looked beyond him.

She'd probably never been on horseback in her life. She was a greenhorn about most ranching matters, and he had to assume that included horses, too. But he didn't care, one way or the other. Riding was only an excuse to be with her again.

Shayla stepped onto the deck, careful to make certain

Honey Girl made it through before letting the screen door swing shut.

"Oh, Ian, what a beautiful animal. But I don't know anything about horses or riding."

"Well, then, I'll have to teach you."

"You would do that?"

"Be glad to, if you're willing."

"Oh, I'm willing. I've *always* wanted to learn to ride." Her eyes twinkled with excitement. "I've just never had the opportunity before. I'd love for you to teach me."

"Then I'm happy to oblige. Come with me. I'll introduce you to Pumpkin. She's as gentle as a lamb. Easiest goin' saddle horse on the place. Perfect for someone's first ride."

"Pumpkin?"

"Don't look at me like that. I didn't name her." He chuckled as they descended the steps, side by side.

"Who did?"

"Joanne."

"Oh. I'm sorry." She looked uncomfortable. "I didn't mean to—"

"It's all right, Shayla. I can talk about Jo."

They arrived at the spot where he had tethered the two horses. Ian took hold of the buckskin's bridle and stroked her muzzle while looking into her intelligent dark brown eyes.

"Pumpkin here was born in the middle of the night during one of the worst spring blizzards this valley's ever seen. It was a difficult birth. We thought we were gonna lose the brood mare. Joanne and I were out in the barn the whole time."

He could see it all in his mind as clearly as if it had happened yesterday instead of over eleven years ago.

"Then the storm snapped some power lines. We scrambled to light several lanterns just before Pumpkin arrived."

He remembered Joanne, kneeling on the stall floor, the collar of her coat turned up, her gloved hands resting on her thighs.

"I guess it was the lantern light, but the filly was the brightest orange color we'd ever seen. Joanne said she looked like a pumpkin in a pumpkin patch. The name stuck."

"And her mother?" Shayla asked. "The brood mare? Was she all right?"

He smiled, liking the tenderheartedness he heard in her voice. "She pulled through. Gave birth to another half-dozen foals before she was put out to pasture."

"Thank goodness."

"Come over here," he said, reaching for her arm and drawing her closer. Then he took her hand and placed it on Pumpkin's neck. "Talk to her. Get acquainted."

"Hello, Pumpkin." Shayla cautiously stroked the mare's neck.

"She's a quarter horse. Eleven years old now. Fourteen hands tall."

"Fourteen hands?"

"A hand is about four inches, and a horse's height is measured from the withers." He touched the ridge between the shoulder bones at the base of the mare's neck. "From right here."

"How tall is your horse?"

"Blue? He's over sixteen hands."

Her gaze moved back and forth between the horses, comparing the two.

For the next fifteen minutes or so, Ian continued his

impromptu teaching session, acquainting her with the conformation of the horse.

He was learning, too. Learning what an apt student Shayla was. Green, maybe, but bright. And particularly pretty in the golden afternoon sunlight, filtering down through the treetops. Today, he noticed, she smelled of vanilla rather than flowers.

Like cookies baking in a warm kitchen.

At the precise moment that particular thought drifted through his mind, he found himself in a prime position to kiss the exposed back of her neck. It would have been easy to lean down and find out for himself if she tasted as good as she smelled.

Luckily, good sense prevailed, and he resisted the temptation. It was too soon, no matter how much he might like to give it a try.

A shiver of awareness ran through Shayla, a tingle that started at her nape, then shot down her spine. Her mouth dry, her heartbeat erratic, she turned to face Ian. For the briefest of moments, she saw the flicker of desire in his eyes. Then it was gone.

Much to her disappointment.

Her heart sank. Her pulse regulated.

"Ready to give it a try?" he asked.

Her pulse quickened again. "Give what a try?"

"A horseback ride."

"Oh." A return of disappointment. She must seem as dumb as a brick. "Sure. I'd love to."

He glanced at her bare legs. "You'll need to change out of those shorts and into some jeans. And some boots, too."

"I don't own any boots. At least, not the cowboy variety."

"Well, then, the ride'll have to wait. Not safe to ride in a saddle without shoes that have a good heel."

Disappointment seemed to be the feeling of the day. And wasn't that for the best? It was only last night that she'd determined she would avoid giving into these feelings.

"Tell you what," he said. "You shop for those boots tomorrow when the store opens, and we'll take a ride in the afternoon before you leave the ranch."

His smile, the look in his eyes, everything about him kept her from refusing. "Okay."

I've got no backbone, she decided after he'd bid her good day and mounted his gelding. *No backbone at all.*

She lifted Honey into her arms before the puppy could follow after the departing horses.

"So much for my resolve. I didn't even make it twenty-four hours. Not a measly twenty-four hours."

She walked toward the cabin, her thoughts still on the tall, dark-haired man astride the gray horse. What she wouldn't have given to own a pair of Western boots. Why on earth hadn't she bought herself a pair before now? She should have known she would need them eventually. This was cowboy country, after all.

And oh, what a cowboy Ian was.

She tried, unsuccessfully, to stop thinking of him, to chase his image from her mind.

"Why did this have to happen to me now? I go for months and months, years even, without noticing a guy. Then I come up here and *wham!*"

Honey whimpered, wriggling madly, trying to get free.

"Big help, you are." She set the puppy down and watched her scamper through the underbrush, chasing a squirrel or chipmunk or something.

The back of Shayla's neck tingled again. She closed her eyes, remembering. She'd thought he was going to kiss her. She'd thought he might pull her against him and kiss her until she went crazy.

That was merely wishful thinking. It had to be. Why would Ian O'Connell, a guy who could have any woman he wanted, just by flashing that great smile of his, want Shayla Vincent? The answer: He wouldn't. She was all wrong for him. And for that matter, he was all wrong for her. Especially now.

"Murder and mayhem," she muttered. "I've got to remember why I'm here. Just to create murder and mayhem on paper."

She whistled for Honey, then took the puppy inside, returning to the computer, to Chet Morrison and his problems with True Barry, a curvaceous, long-legged, gorgeous femme fatale, if ever there was one.

Exactly the sort of woman Shayla wished she could be for Ian.

The next morning found Ian eager to get his chores done so he could give Shayla her next lesson. It was all he'd thought about last night before going to bed, and it was the first thought he'd had upon awakening this morning.

"Ty, I want you and Mick to ride over to Silver Ridge this morning." Ian flipped the left stirrup over the saddle and tightened the cinch. "I want to know how the water's holding up over there."

"The water? What makes you think there'd be a problem at Silver Ridge? Those water holes haven't run dry in all the years you been running cattle there. Not even in the worst drought years."

He didn't look up. "Something's just been nagging at

me. Don't know what exactly. Call it a hunch." *Call it Shayla Vincent,* would have been a more honest response. "Better safe than sorry."

Ty grunted. "Whatever you say. You're the boss."

Darn right, he was the boss. But more important, the ride to Silver Ridge would keep Ty out until after six o'clock. Plenty of time to serve Ian's purposes.

Okay, he thought as he mounted the palomino gelding he was riding today. So maybe it wasn't fair, getting Ty as far away from Shayla as possible. But they said all was fair in love and war.

He whistled for his trusty collies, then rode south, following the trail between rolling pastureland and pine-covered mountainside. He would have preferred to remain at the house until Shayla arrived, but he had to locate and drive in some strays before he could take the rest of the day off to spend with her.

He grinned, imagining Shayla in a tight pair of Levi's and a sleeveless Western shirt, the type the women's shop on Main Street kept in stock. She would look real cute in those clothes. Come to think of it, she looked real cute in those old cutoffs and baggy T-shirts of hers.

The night of the dance she'd looked more than cute. She'd looked pretty, even...sexy.

His grin broadened. Exactly when was it, he wondered, that she'd gone from being odd to sexy?

He laughed aloud before nudging his horse into a canter.

The worst of the cleanup was behind Shayla. Once she got the master bedroom uncluttered, dusted and vacuumed and the master bath scoured, it wouldn't be all that hard to keep the house tidy from week to week. Even cleaning only on Mondays and Thursdays, as was her plan. From here on out, Ian's mother could come for that visit, and he wouldn't have to be afraid of disappointing her.

She set her cleaning supplies on the floor, then made a quick survey of the bedroom. As with most of the other rooms in the house, she found an abundance of magazines, some several years old.

''Doesn't he throw *anything* away?''

In addition to magazines, she discovered about a dozen volumes on animal husbandry. Books on cattle breeding, horse training, wildlife management, farming procedures and more. But what surprised her most was the oversize copy of the complete works of Shakespeare. She wouldn't have thought Ian interested in the Bard.

Maybe the book had belonged to Joanne.

Joanne.

She turned and began visually searching the bedroom for a photograph of Ian's wife. She wanted to see what the woman had looked like. She wasn't disappointed. She found a collection of framed photos on the bureau. There was one of his parents; she could tell it was them because of the man's striking resemblance to Ian. There was another of his parents with him and his sister when the children were small. There was a large photo of his sister and her family at the ocean. There was another of Ian on horseback.

But it was the photograph of Joanne and Ian on their wedding day that Shayla reached for, her gaze fastened on the bride.

Joanne looked incredibly young, her eyes full of excitement, innocence, anticipation and hope. She was tall and slender, exquisitely beautiful with high cheekbones and delicately chiseled features. She was the type of woman who grew prettier with every passing year.

In the photo, Ian was staring at his bride with a look of love so profound, so intense, it made Shayla's heart ache to see it.

No wonder he'd never married again. A love that strong surely lasted forever.

Suddenly she felt intrusive. It was wrong to be looking at this photo and wishing....

Wishing what? That she was as tall and slender and beautiful as Joanne O'Connell? Well, that was never going to happen. Nor was it possible Joanne's husband would one day look at Shayla in that same way.

And that was really what she'd been wishing, way down deep in the most secret corner of her heart.

She set the photo back with the others, wanting to forget she'd allowed such wishful thoughts to surface.

"Just get your work done and go home," she said aloud. "You don't belong here. You're just the housekeeper and will never be anything more. You don't even *want* to be anything more."

A new pair of boots, plus an older, well-worn, comfortable pair of jeans, were out in her car. She was supposed to have a riding lesson this afternoon. She mustn't do it. She must leave before he returned. It would be crazy for her to stay, to let herself hope.

Her family already thought her certifiable for coming to Idaho. If she fell for Ian, not only would she lose sight of her purpose for moving here, she would also be proving her family right.

Because falling for a man who was still in love with his dead wife would certainly be an insane thing for her to do.

It was a hot June day, the absence of a breeze intensifying the strength of the sun.

Ian knew it would be more humane, both for the animals and for himself, to slow down a bit, but he didn't do it. He drove his horse and the cattle relentlessly, determined to get back to the house before Shayla could leave.

Instinct told him she *would* leave if he wasn't there to keep her from it. He wasn't certain why he felt that way. He just did.

By the time he herded the strays into the corral and closed the gate, sweat was streaming down his spine. Ian could taste grime on his tongue, and he figured he didn't smell much better than his horse.

But all that was important to him at the moment was that Shayla's car was still parked in front of his house.

He dismounted and looped the reins around a post, then strode toward the front door. He arrived on the porch just as the door opened. There she was, car keys in hand, trying to make her getaway, as he'd suspected she might.

"Hi." He casually blocked her way while giving her a warm smile.

"Hello." Her expression said she hadn't expected him back this soon.

"You aren't leaving. You didn't forget your riding lesson, did you?"

She glanced toward the car, and he could tell she was warring within herself, trying to decide what to do, how to answer.

He took another step toward her. "I've been looking forward to this all morning."

"You have?" Surprise leapt into her eyes as she stared at him.

"Yes." He paused, then asked, "Did you buy some boots?"

She nodded.

"Great." His grin broadened. "If you don't mind, I'll take a quick shower, grab a bite to eat and then we can begin. Sound like a plan?"

Once more she glanced toward her car. Once more she nodded. "All right. I…I'll fix us some sandwiches while you wash up."

The desire to kiss her rushed back. It would be so easy to do. One long step would take him to her. His hands could close around her arms, below her shoulders, and he could draw her up onto her tiptoes while he leaned down. Her mouth would probably stay parted, just as it was at this moment.

Would she taste of vanilla? Like cookies baking in a warm kitchen on a summer day? Or was that merely the illusion her cologne cast over him?

Her eyes widened. He saw her swallow hard, watched as she moistened her lips with the tip of her tongue, apparently unaware what that did to him, unaware how such a small act could fan the flames of his desire.

Abruptly she turned and walked into the house, hurrying to the kitchen. Hiding from him, he realized. Afraid of what she'd seen in his eyes.

She was as skittish as a colt. He wanted to know why. He wanted to understand lots of things about her.

Beginning today.

Chapter Eight

She was in trouble. *Big* trouble.

Shayla stood in the center of the large kitchen, her heart hammering, her body quivering. She wasn't mistaken. He'd thought about kissing her. If she hadn't turned away, he might have done it.

And then what?

Heartbreak, that's what.

Letting herself care for this hunk of a cowboy had heartbreak written all over it. Did she want to be a substitute for the woman he loved? No. She'd been settling for second best for far too many years. She'd been taking care of the needs of others for most of her life. Now it was *her* time. Hers!

Oh, but she'd wanted his kisses. She'd wanted to step up close to him, press herself against his body and melt into his embrace. She'd wanted to know his caresses. She'd wanted…

She heard the shower running.

Leave now! her mind screamed. Get out while you can.

But her feet felt as if they'd been nailed to the floor. She couldn't move, couldn't run.

She breathed deeply, then released it, reminding herself it was only a riding lesson she was waiting for. Nothing more. Just a lesson.

The telephone rang. Ian had told her to answer it whenever she was in the house alone. On the fourth ring, she decided to pick it up.

"Hello?"

There was a lengthy hesitation before a woman said, "I'm sorry. I must have dialed the wrong number."

"Wait. Were you calling the O'Connell ranch?"

"Yes." Another pause. "Is Ian there?"

"Yes, he is. I'll see if he's available." She laid the handset on the kitchen counter, then returned to the front of the house, pausing at the base of the stairs. "Ian?" She thought the water had stopped running. "Ian?"

A few moments later, she heard the creak of an opening door. "Yeah?"

"Telephone for you."

"Thanks. I'll get it up here."

She hurried back to the kitchen and discreetly hung up the telephone, resisting the temptation to listen and perhaps discover the woman's identity. It wasn't any of her business. And she would rather eat crushed glass than admit she felt a twinge of jealousy.

As if she had any right to feel such a thing.

"He is only a friend," she reminded herself. "And there is nothing wrong with having a male friend. I am perfectly capable of setting boundaries and sticking to them. No kissing, no hugging and no more dancing. The last thing I want is a fling, and that's all it would be. I'm not his type, and he certainly isn't mine."

She crossed the room to look out the window toward the barn, thinking how pleasant it would be to spend the afternoon with him. Just the two of them. Alone.

"But I am *not* lonely. I like being on my own. I like having a place all to myself. I want to write books. I just want to write my stories. That's what's important to me now."

She drew in a deep breath, then let it out slowly. There. That was better. She was her calm, collected self again. No more wild thoughts.

Her newfound self-control lasted about fifteen seconds.

What would it be like to be loved by a man like Ian? she wondered. Then a quiver ran through her as she silently answered her own question: It would be heaven on earth.

"That was my sister."

She jumped at the sound of Ian's voice, whirling around to face him as he entered the kitchen. His hair was damp, his jaw freshly shaved. He looked relaxed and handsome. Much *too* handsome. Her rebellious heart quickened at the mere sight of him.

"Your sister?" she echoed.

"On the phone. Leigh. My sister in Florida. I told you about her."

"Oh. Yes." She wondered if he'd guessed how curious she was when she'd heard his sister's voice.

"Did you make the sandwiches?" He glanced at the kitchen counter, then back to her.

Had he guessed she'd felt jealous at the possibility of another woman in his life?

He raised an eyebrow as he met her gaze. "The sandwiches?" he repeated.

"No." She shook her head, hoping he hadn't noticed her flushed cheeks. "No, I didn't make them yet. I was just about to start."

"Well, I'd better help you. We need to eat something before we go. We might be out for two or three hours."

"Two or three hours?" She sounded like a parrot, the way she repeated everything he said. What was the matter with her?

He opened the refrigerator. "Yeah. I thought I'd take you over to Elk Flat. It's an easy trail, and it's got mighty pretty scenery. We won't want to rush."

"I hadn't planned to be out that long. I still need to write this afternoon."

It was the truth. It was also an excuse. But for herself or for him, she couldn't be certain.

"I've heard you creative types need to refill the well every so often." He straightened, lunch meat and sandwich spread in his hands. "This'll do you good. I promise."

I doubt that, she thought as she returned his gaze.

But she stayed, just as she'd known all along she would.

Shayla was a natural with horses. She showed no fear once she was in the saddle. Of course it helped that Pumpkin was the most docile horse on the place.

After giving Shayla a brief refresher, Ian had enough confidence in both her and the mare to leave the ranch house behind and head up the trail.

They rode in companionable silence for quite a spell, Shayla observing the scenery and Ian observing Shayla.

Her new duds—felt cowboy hat, shiny black boots

and a shirt the same dark blue as her eyes—almost shouted, *Greenhorn!* Especially the shirt that was trimmed with long, white fringe, both front and back. Patsy Whitehall, who owned the women's clothing shop in town, must have seen her coming from a mile away.

But Ian thought she looked mighty cute in it all the same.

"It's the shirt, isn't it?"

He grinned but didn't answer.

"I knew it was a bad choice." She glanced over at him. "The fringe, right?"

He shrugged, trying not to laugh.

"I thought so. I looked at myself in the mirror and thought, this is only for rodeo queens and country-western bars. Don't buy it. But I did."

Now he laughed.

"I knew it, but I just couldn't help myself." She returned his smile, then joined his laughter with her own. "I guess I wanted to be Dale Evans," she added after she caught her breath again.

"Don't feel too badly. You wouldn't be the first."

"I suppose not." Her smile faded as their gazes held.

The desire to kiss her returned. If he reached for Pumpkin's reins, he could draw both horses to a halt and then...

Shayla glanced away.

"Tell me about the book you're writing," he said, hoping to make her look at him again.

She didn't.

"Have you killed anyone this week?" he persisted.

That did the trick.

Mischief sparked in her eyes as their gazes met. "As a matter of fact, I'm just about ready for my third corpse."

"Male or female?"

"Definitely male. A clothing critic, I think."

"Knife?"

"Pistol. Easier to ambush someone. Especially if he's riding alone out on some trail…like this one, for instance."

"Did I mention how much I like your shirt, Miss Vincent? Especially that fancy white fringe. Real attractive, if you ask me."

She laughed again.

It was the prettiest sound he'd ever heard.

"You are an extremely wise man, Mr. O'Connell. Extremely wise."

"Thanks, ma'am. I do what I can." He winked at her, then turned serious. "Now, tell me more about your book."

"Are you really interested?"

She might as well have said no one had ever cared enough to ask before. He could see it in her eyes, hear it in her voice. It made him angry at her friends and family, people he'd never met. People who should have known better, just as he should have known better with Joanne.

It was a mistake he would never make again.

"Yeah," he answered at long last. "I'm really interested."

"I'm not sure what to tell you. I've never…talked to anyone about my writing before. I'm just learning it all myself. Everyday I discover something new about the process."

"Tell me where you get your ideas."

A flicker of a smile curved her mouth as she turned her gaze up the trail. "Everywhere." She made a sweeping motion with her right hand. "They're all around me.

Sometimes it seems like my head will burst, it's so full of them. Everything I see and hear. Everything I read. Everyone I meet. It's like having other people living in your head, talking to you." She flushed. "You must think I'm crazy."

Ian suppressed a grin of his own, afraid she would look at him and think he was laughing at her. But he wasn't. "No, I don't think you're crazy." *In fact, I think you're wonderful,* he added silently. "Go on. Tell me more."

By the time the two of them reached Elk Flat, Shayla had told Ian more about her book than she'd ever imagined she could share with someone. It took her by surprise, how easy it was to tell him her ideas, to talk about her characters and her plot. He made her forget her usual reticence. With his carefully interspersed questions, he also made her forget her fears of having to return to Portland a failure, proving all the doubters right. Instead, his interest made her feel as if she had already succeeded.

As the trail came out of the dense forest, opening up into a huge meadow, Ian drew back on the reins and softly announced, "This is what I hoped you'd get to see. It's why I left the dogs in their kennels."

A herd of elk raised their heads in unison, watchful of the human trespassers but not frightened away as yet. A stag with an enormous rack stared directly at Shayla.

She drew an awestruck breath. "Oh my."

"That's just how I feel when I see them," Ian whispered.

"What a beautiful sight."

"They feed here the better part of the summer."

"I've never seen elk outside of a zoo."

"This is how they ought to be seen. Wild and free."

She looked at him. "You love it here. This land. Nature. Everything. It's a part of you, isn't it?"

"Yes." He met her gaze. "I've never wanted to live anywhere else. Never wanted to *be* anything else than just exactly what I am. I love the business of ranching, working outdoors, the animals. All of it. It's hard work, but it's worth it."

"I can see why you'd feel that way. About Paradise Ranch, I mean. Why would anyone want to leave when there's so much beauty all around?"

Something in the way he studied her made her stomach flutter. There seemed to be a question written in his eyes, something she couldn't quite understand.

He glanced away, then said, "Let's walk awhile. My legs could use a stretch before we start back." He dismounted, then waited for her to do the same.

Remembering his earlier instructions, Shayla gripped the saddle horn with her left hand, swung her right leg over Pumpkin's rump and eased herself to the ground. She was feeling a bit of pride in her ability to do it without any help or additional tutoring. The feeling disappeared the moment her right knee started to buckle beneath her.

"Easy there." Ian's hand gripped her arm, keeping her upright while she steadied herself.

Heat rose in her cheeks. She hadn't wanted to look like an amateur in front of him. He did everything so easily, so perfectly. So...

She looked up, found him watching her, felt her insides twist into a knot.

Before she knew what was happening, he leaned down and his mouth briefly captured hers. What strength the ride on horseback hadn't sapped from her legs, his kiss did.

He straightened and took a step backward, but his eyes remained locked with hers and his hand still gripped her arm.

"Why did you do that?" she whispered, touching her lips with her fingertips.

"Why do you think?"

"I...I don't know."

He drew close, cupping her chin with the callused fingers of one hand, forcing her to continue to meet his intense gaze. "Because I wondered if you would taste as sweet as you look." He lowered his voice. "And you do."

It was a ridiculous thing for him to say. A man like Ian with a woman like her? It didn't happen. Not in real life. He could have any woman he wanted. A beauty queen. A movie star. A cover girl.

He kissed her again. Slowly this time.

She closed her eyes and instinctively leaned into him. She knew she had to be dreaming. Therefore she might as well enjoy it while it lasted.

She would awaken soon enough.

Ian knew this wasn't a dream.

Everything he was feeling was real—and more intense than he'd anticipated it would be. Wisdom and caution demanded that he end the kiss before he did something really stupid.

Like ask her to stay in Rainbow Valley forever, to put up with the long winters and the hot summers. Like ask her to never return to Portland and her parents and brothers and sisters. Like ask her to marry him and share his home. Like ask her to be the mother of his children.

Not just stupid. *Insane!* A sane man didn't think about proposing to a woman he'd known such a short time. A sane man took his time, made sure he'd found the right woman. A sane man didn't rush in where angels feared to tread.

He released her and stepped away, putting some distance between them. Otherwise he knew it wouldn't be long before he'd want to kiss her again.

"We'd better start back." Repressed desire made his voice sound gruff.

"Yes." She turned her back toward him, once again gripping the saddle horn. "Let's go."

"Shayla—"

"Don't say anything. Let's just pretend this never happened."

"But—"

"Please, Ian."

Through the fever of his own wants and desires, he heard the hurt in her voice. Something warned him that he'd better go slowly or lose whatever hope he had of making her feel for him what he was feeling for her.

And sane or crazy, he *was* feeling it.

Ian O'Connell was falling in love.

The telephone company installed Shayla's phone the next afternoon. Needing to get her thoughts off of Ian and onto something else, she dialed Portland, certain her family could be counted on to succeed where she had failed.

"Oh, honey," her mother said, "it's good to hear your voice. You didn't call last week, and we were getting worried."

"Sorry, Mom. I've been busy. But my phone's in now. Let me give you my number."

Reba Vincent repeated the number as she wrote it down. When she was finished, she asked, "Now tell me what's kept you so busy you couldn't call home and keep me from worrying about you."

"My writing mostly."

"And what else?"

Shayla felt a sting of disappointment. She'd harbored a secret hope that her mother would ask how the book was going, that she would express interest—just as Ian had done yesterday.

Heat rushed through her as she recalled for about the hundredth time the way he'd kissed her, the way standing so close to him had caused her heart to thrum and her blood to boil. How it had weakened her knees...not to mention her brain.

"Shayla dear, are you still there?"

She gave her head a quick shake. "Yes, Mom, I'm here. What did you say?"

"I asked what you've been doing with all your free time. Heaven knows, I can't imagine. There's nothing in Rainbow Valley, as I remember. Not even a movie theater."

"Well, for one thing, I've got a job."

"A job? Doing what?"

"I'm working part-time as a housekeeper for a neighbor. And he's going to make some repairs to the cabin."

"A housekeeper?" Reba let out a long, disheartened sigh. "That's a horrible waste of your skills. I do wish you'd come back to Portland. I know you could find decent employment if you would only try. Besides, I can't bear to think of you living in that horrible cabin."

"But it isn't horrible, Mom. It's wonderful. And yesterday, I went for a horseback ride with a neighbor and saw a herd of elk and—"

"Sis!" an excited voice interrupted. Olivia had obviously picked up the extension. "Is that you?"

"It's me."

"You'll never guess who asked me out on a date. Go on. Try. You'll never guess."

By the time Shayla hung up the phone twenty minutes later, she'd learned the answer to Olivia's question—she'd been asked out by the star quarterback and high school heartthrob. She'd also learned that her youngest sister Crystal had garnered a spot on the junior high swim team, her brother Dwight had been promoted at work, her sister Anne had been asked to oversee a church fund-raiser, her brother Ken had moved into an apartment with one of his college buddies, and her youngest brother George was now bagging groceries at the nearby supermarket.

But no one had asked Shayla about her novel.

She sat on the sofa, staring at the telephone in its cradle, resentment flooding her chest. She knew they missed her. Everyone had said so. And yet not one of them seemed to care about what mattered so very much to her.

Why couldn't they be like Ian?

Oh, no. She didn't want to go there. Just the thought of his name, and she was once again remembering the way he'd held and kissed her yesterday. She knew it was only because he was lonely. Ty had told her that Ian hadn't had a girlfriend in at least a year. And she could tell he still mourned the wife he'd lost a decade before. Of course he was lonely.

"And I'm handy," she whispered.

She rose from the sofa and walked to the mirror she'd hung at the end of the hall, staring hard at her reflection. Short and pudgy. A mop of the most unruly hair God had ever created. Round cheeks that reminded her of a squirrel with a mouth full of acorns. Not as ugly as a mud fence, perhaps, but certainly nothing special to look at, either.

She remembered the wedding photograph. Joanne had been a striking, classic beauty. Tall and slender and everything else that Shayla wasn't.

No, there was no way Ian could be attracted to her after being married to a woman like Joanne. He might like Shayla. He might want to be her friend and spend time with her. He might even want to do more than just kiss her. But if so, it was only because he was lonely for female company and she happened to be available.

Turning away from the mirror, she said, "I'm not falling into that trap. I won't do it. So help me, Hannah, I won't."

And yet, despite her determination to control the direction of her thoughts, she kept remembering the way Ian had asked questions about her writing, her characters and her plot, the way he'd sounded interested in every detail she'd shared, the way he'd watched her, the way he'd smiled. She kept remembering the way he'd kissed her, the feel of his body—strong and muscular—so close to her own. She remembered that he'd smelled of aftershave, dust and leather. A strangely appealing combination of scents, now that she thought about it.

A groan slipped up from her chest. "I've got to get to work. I've got to quit thinking about Ian. And that's final."

Chapter Nine

Leigh called again the following Sunday.

"Mom said to tell you she'll come and stay at the ranch for the month of October. Do you think you can get along with the girls on your own until then?"

"Of course," he answered, sounding more confident than he felt. "How hard can it be?"

Her soft laughter didn't do much to reassure him.

"Listen, there are plenty of folks around the valley who'll be glad to give me advice if I need it." He immediately thought of Shayla. "My neighbor, the one living in the old Erickson place, is the oldest of seven kids. I can always ask her what to do if I don't know."

"Is that the woman who answered your phone last week when I called?"

"Yes, that's her."

"Hmm."

He could almost see the wheels turning in his sister's head.

"Anything I should know about her?" she finally asked, sounding both curious and amused.

"Not at the moment. No." But he was hoping there would be.

Not that he was having a great deal of luck in that department. Ever since the day he'd kissed her, Shayla had avoided him like the plague. It was as obvious as the nose on her face that she didn't want to be alone with him. It would have been plenty easy to assume she disliked him.

Only he remembered too well how soft and pliable her mouth had been beneath his. He hadn't imagined her response to his kisses. Whatever the reason was that she wanted to avoid him, it wasn't because she wasn't attracted to him.

Now all he had to do was figure out what obstacle he had to overcome, and then overcome it. And he *would* succeed.

"Hello? Ian? Oh blast. Jim, I think I've been disconnected. Ian, are you there?"

"I'm here, Leigh," he answered. "Sorry. I got distracted by something. Tell me again what you were saying."

"Well, please listen this time."

"I'm listening. You've got my full attention. Honest."

"Write this down so you don't forget. We'll be arriving in Boise on the twenty-ninth. That's a Tuesday." She gave him the airline, flight number and arrival time. "Jim and I won't be able to go up to the ranch with you and the girls like we'd originally planned. We have to fly over to Seattle the next morning. The company has accelerated everything. We'll be shipping most of the girls' things directly to the ranch, but we'll pack enough for them to get by until the rest is delivered.''

"Won't need much until school starts. Boots, jeans, shorts, swimsuits. It's summer, Leigh. You know what summers are like up here. Lazy, hazy, crazy, just like the song says.''

"Oh, I do wish we could stay with you for a few days. At least until they settle in and begin to feel comfortable. It's going to be such a change for them, and they only barely remember you from your last visit to Florida.''

He tipped his chair back on its hind legs until his shoulders touched the wall. "You gotta quit worrying. Cathy and Angie and I are going to get along fine. They'll miss you, but I won't let them have much time to stew over it.''

"They're only six years old.''

"When you and I were six, we were helping Dad round up cattle. You could catch and clean a brook trout all by yourself. At least you always bragged that you could.''

"They're city kids, Ian.''

"That'll change.''

There was a slightly choked sound in her voice as she said, "I'm going to miss them so much. They grow up so fast. Maybe I shouldn't go. Maybe I should stay in the States and—''

"Leigh, you know you want to be with Jim. This will be an experience of a lifetime for you both. Will you just trust me to keep those kids safe and happy? They'll be loved and cared for. You've got my word on it.''

Somehow, by the time they rang off, he managed to convince his sister everything would be okay. Now if only he was as confident as he'd sounded.

Grabbing his hat from the peg on the wall near the door, he went outside. As the screen door swung shut with a high-pitched squeak, Coira and Bonny came racing toward him from around the far side of the barn. He gave each of them a pat on the head before striding across the barnyard to the paddock where he stood looking at the horses that were grazing within.

Well, there was no point kidding himself. He wanted to see Shayla. He was tired of her efforts to avoid him. Now he only needed to decide between saddling up a horse or driving over in his truck. It was going to be one or the other.

A few moments later, he'd made up his mind. He would drive. It was faster.

"You might as well be straight with me." Ty tipped his hat back on his head and stared at Shayla with a piercing gaze. "Won't go no further than here."

She looked down at the glass of lemonade in her hand. "Of course I like Ian. He's been a great neighbor. Very helpful." She motioned toward the cabin. "Look at all he's accomplished already."

"That's not what I meant, and you know it."

She gave a helpless little shrug.

"Look, I don't reckon there's any man I like and respect more'n Ian. He's my friend. And I know he's got a hankerin' for you—"

"A hankerin'?" she interrupted, amused by his word choice but not the meaning.

"Darn right, a hankerin'. And unless I missed my guess, you're feeling the same way about him. So I just want to know if I need to clear out. No point standin' in the way of two folk who want the same thing. Now is there?"

"No, I don't suppose there is." She met his gaze again. "But you're wrong about it being more than friendship between Ian and me."

He glanced down the road leading from the highway. "Am I?" A grin curved his mouth.

She followed his gaze and saw the teal pickup, followed by a rising cloud of dust.

"Looks like Ian wouldn't agree with you."

Conflicting emotions—joy, despair, hope, disappointment—raged in her chest. She'd evaded him all week just so she wouldn't have to feel these things. And now he'd come to see her.

Ty set aside the glass of lemonade she'd given him a few minutes before. "I think I'll be heading into town." He bent his hat brim in her direction. "You take care, Shayla. You hear?"

He went to his Jeep, waiting beside it until Ian pulled into the drive and brought his rig to a halt. Then Ty called out a greeting to his friend before getting into his own vehicle and driving away.

With her heart tattooing in her chest, Shayla watched as Ian strode toward the cabin, his expression grim.

When their gazes met, he asked, "Did I interrupt something?"

"No." Ian is just a friend, she reminded herself.

He glanced over his shoulder. "Ty's got too much free time," he grumbled.

He almost sounded jealous—which was about the most ridiculous notion she'd ever had.

"Shayla, we need to talk." He came up the steps. "About what happened last week. Up at Elk Flat."

"I'd rather not."

"Well, I think we should."

With a sigh escaping her lips, she crossed to the opposite side of the deck.

He wasn't deterred. "Look, we're both adults. Why are we acting like a couple of teenagers with their first crush?"

Good question.

"I like you, Shayla. A lot, as it turns out."

That caused her to turn around.

He took a step toward her. He was holding his hat in his hands. "I'd just like to know if you might be feeling a bit of the same way about me. If not, then we'll forget I kissed you. But if you are, then I'd like to see where this thing might lead."

"It won't lead us to bed. I'll tell you that right now."

For some reason, her comment caused him to smile.

"Do you think I'm kidding?" she asked sharply. "I'm not. The last thing I want or need is a lover, Mr. O'Connell. It's not my style."

His grin vanished. He took another step forward. "Believe it or not, Miss Vincent, I'm an old-fashioned kind of guy. I'm not asking you to go to bed with me. I believe in the love and marriage stuff *before* sex. It's how I was raised and how I plan to raise my kids, if ever I'm lucky enough to have any." He raised his voice another notch. "So you can put those big-city thoughts right out of that pretty little head of yours."

She stared at him, wide-eyed. Never in her wildest dreams would she have expected a man to say what Ian had just said to her. She'd heard a few arguments for why she *should* go to bed with some guy, but she'd never heard one telling her why he wasn't going to take her there.

Ian raked his fingers through his thick, dark hair. "And that's not to say I don't find you attractive as all-get-out.'' One more step brought him to her, forcing her to look up to meet his gaze. He continued, more softly now. ''I *do* find you attractive. You're all I can think about lately. So do I have no more chance with you than a one-legged man at a kickin' contest? Or can I come callin' on you now and again?''

One-legged man at a kicking contest? Come calling on her?

She couldn't help it. She giggled.

He took immediate affront. ''I see,'' he said stiffly, then turned. ''I'll be on my way.''

''No!'' She grabbed his arm. ''Don't go. It wasn't…I wasn't…'' She slipped around him so that she could see his face again. ''Please don't go. I wasn't laughing at you. Honestly, I wasn't. It's just—''

He kissed her, silencing whatever else she might have said. And whatever that was, it was quickly forgotten. Her brain went numb and her senses went into overdrive. She was aware of his work-roughened hands cradling the sides of her face and his sun-chapped lips against hers. She was keenly aware of his warm, masculine scent, the hard beat of his heart against her chest and the full length of his rock-solid body.

By the time he released her, she had to grab for the deck railing in order to steady herself.

Ian slapped his Stetson onto his head. ''I reckon I got my answer.''

I reckon you did, she thought to herself, too breathless to speak.

''I'd like to take you to supper tomorrow night, if you'd be kind enough to accept my invitation. There's a nice Italian restaurant in McCall. Won't take us too long to drive over there. We can dine on the deck overlooking the lake. It's nice this time of year. Not too hot and still early in the season for the mosquitoes to be bothersome. I'll have you home by eleven at the latest.''

How did words like *reckon* and *dine* fit in the same guy's vocabulary? One minute he sounded like he was straight out of some old dime novel and the next he sounded as cosmopolitan as any man she'd ever met in a corporate setting.

So who was Ian O'Connell anyway, and why was he attracted to her?

''Is that a yes, Miss Vincent?''

Helplessly she nodded.

''I'll come for you at five o'clock.''

Another nod.

''Evening, Shayla.'' He brushed her cheek with another kiss, then strode away.

''You've got it bad for her,'' Ty said the next morning as he and Ian stretched a new section of barbed wire between the fence posts.

Ian didn't try to deny it.

''I'd just about given up hope you'd ever find somebody who'd make you feel this way.''

''That makes two of us.''

Not that Ian thought it was a smart thing, letting himself fall for Shayla Vincent. All the signs were there, saying this wasn't something that would work. She didn't know squat about ranch work or cattle or horses. Oh, sure, she could learn. She was nobody's fool. But she'd spent her whole life in a big city and was like a fish out of water in Rainbow Valley. Let that first hard winter roll around when they wouldn't be able to get out of the ranch for weeks at a time. Let her get fed up with the limited selection of items at the small grocery store in town. Let her want to go back to Portland for a visit with her family and have to endure the long drive to Boise, just to catch a plane, a plane that could be grounded for any number of reasons. Let her be dying to see the hot new movie and have to wait for weeks before it made it to the theater in McCall where movies were only shown on Fridays and Saturdays for most of the year.

Those things drove the flatlanders crazy.

But he'd be doggoned if seeing the signs made any difference to him. He'd already lost his heart, pure and simple. He'd probably lost it the very first time he'd seen her, marching around on the deck with that trick knife of hers. He'd thought her mighty odd, and yet, even then…

"So what're you gonna do about it?" Ty asked, dragging Ian from his private thoughts.

He straightened, met the younger cowboy's gaze and grinned. "Every dang thing I can."

"I got a feelin' it won't take much."

"Sure hope you're right, Ty."

"Believe me, if she'd given me the time of day, I wouldn't've given up so easy. There's something real special about that one."

Ian laughed as he pulled off his work gloves. "Don't I know it."

"Reckon you do." Ty swept off his hat and wiped the sweat from his brow with his shirtsleeve. "It's gonna be a scorcher today. Let's get that next section done before it gets any hotter."

Ty was right. The day did turn into a scorcher.

By the time Ian stepped into the shower that afternoon, the weatherman on the radio was saying a new record high had been set for this date. Luckily for Ian, his pickup had air-conditioning. He and Shayla would keep cool during the drive to McCall.

Cool? He never felt cool when he was with Shayla. Just thinking about her caused a fever in his blood. She had him cinched to the last hole, and that was the truth.

What he wouldn't give to be able to take her into his arms right now and kiss her until she dropped. And where he'd like to drop her was right into the bed next to him.

After all, old-fashioned didn't mean dead.

The words hadn't come right all day long. Crinkled paper surrounded Shayla's chair. Sheets and sheets of twenty-pound bond. The printer had spewed them forth, then Shayla had decided they weren't good enough to line the bottom of a bird cage.

The problem was with True Barry. She was supposed to be the next murder victim, but suddenly, Chet had developed more than a passing interest in the woman. Maybe True wasn't such a liar. Maybe she wasn't a tramp. Maybe she wasn't deserving of death. Maybe she should have the chance to fall in love with a good and decent guy like Chet Morrison.

Shayla pressed her forehead against the computer screen and released a groan. "I'm not writing a romance. This is a mystery, for crying out loud."

But who said there couldn't be love in a mystery novel?

"Focus," she muttered. "I've got to focus."

She should be concentrating on red herrings, believable motivations and hidden clues. Instead, she had written about how sexy True looked in that little red number and how much Chet wanted to kiss her. In fact, it looked like the two of them might get swept away by their passions and…

"Oh, for pity's sake!" She rolled her chair back from her desk and got up, kicking at the pile of papers around her feet. "At this rate I'll never get the book written."

Still muttering to herself, she walked toward the kitchen, thinking it might help if she fixed herself a sandwich. Her stomach had been growling for at least half an hour, if not more. She'd better have some lunch.

Then her gaze fell on the clock above the stove, and she nearly had heart failure—4:50? But it couldn't be! The last time she'd checked the time, it hadn't even been noon.

"No, no, no!"

She rushed to the bedroom. She didn't dare glance at the mirror as she whisked her T-shirt over her head and dropped it, alongside her cutoffs, onto the floor. She wished there was time to take a shower and do something special with her hair, but it was too late for that.

Oh, how had she let this happen to her? She'd wanted to look her best for this date.

Though why it should matter so much, she couldn't say. She wasn't fooling herself. Ian's attraction for her was a temporary thing. He might not realize it yet, but she did. He was lonely. Ty had as much as told her so. And lonely men were willing to spend time with women like Shayla until someone prettier or smarter or more successful came along. And then they weren't lonely anymore.

But still…

She dressed quickly in a loose-flowing, sleeveless summer dress. Then she ran a quick brush through her hair before twisting it into a roll and catching it with a hair claw at the back of her head. Finally she applied a bit of makeup, despairing that it would not make one shred of difference.

She wished she was tall and beautiful like True Barry. But True was a fictional character and could be changed with a bit of typing on the keyboard. Shayla was stuck with who and what she was.

A knock sounded at her open front door.

"Just a moment!" she called out. Then she took one last look at herself in the mirror, sighed and hurried out of the bathroom.

Ian smiled when he saw her.

Shayla's stomach did a cartwheel.

"Hi." His voice was low, his eyes appreciative.

"Hi." She felt like a teenager about to go to her first prom.

"You ready?"

"Yes." She reached for her purse.

He motioned for her to come outside. After she did so, he closed the door behind her.

"Hope you're hungry," he said as he took hold of her arm and guided her down the steps. "The restaurant I'm taking you to has great food. Italian. Seafood. Steaks. Salads."

Only ten minutes before, she'd thought she was ravenous. But she didn't think she could eat a bite now.

He helped her into the pickup, but before he closed the door he said, "You look pretty as a picture, Shayla."

She almost believed him.

"Thanks," Ian whispered several hours later as they stood on her deck in the pale light of the last quarter moon. "I had a great time."

"So did I," she confessed, knowing she'd never spoken truer words to anyone.

"I enjoyed hearing more about your family. I'll bet they're fun to be around."

"They'd like you, too."

"I wish Leigh and Jim could meet you before they leave for the Mideast." He leaned closer.

She could smell his aftershave, a musky scent that made her go all soft and fluttery inside. "The Mideast?"

"Didn't I tell you?" His breath was warm on her forehead. "I thought I did. Jim's job is taking him overseas for a year."

"Oh." She sighed as her eyes drifted closed, knowing he was about to kiss her.

And he did, tenderly plying her mouth with his. She'd never been kissed the way Ian kissed her now. Like she was precious, fragile, beautiful.

She wished the evening never had to end.

It seemed a wonderful lifetime later that he raised his head, ending the sweet agony. She opened her eyes, gazed up at him. "Would you like to come in for a while? I could make some decaf."

"I probably shouldn't," he replied huskily.

It gave her a small thrill, hearing the desire in his voice.

"Well...maybe just for one cup." He kissed her again.

A few minutes later, Shayla lifted the lid off the can of decaffeinated coffee with shaking fingertips. She wondered if Ian had any idea what he did to her, then decided he must know. And best of all, she was certain she had the same effect on him.

The telephone's sharp peal jerked her from her pleasantly tortured reverie. It was almost midnight. Alarm darted through her as she reached to answer it.

"Hello?"

"Shayla!"

"Anne? What's wrong?"

"Shayla, I need to come stay with you. Oh, please don't say no. Please."

Her sister was crying, making it difficult to understand what she was saying. "Calm down, Anne."

"I can't bear to stay here. Not another minute."

"What happened?"

Out of the corner of her eye, she saw Ian rise from the sofa and move toward her.

"I…I can't talk about it right now. I just need to get away from Portland. Please let me come to stay with you. I promise I won't get in the way."

It had to have something to do with her latest boyfriend. Anne always overreacted when something went awry in her love life.

"Anne, there really isn't a lot of room in the cabin. My computer is in the living room and I—"

"I don't know what I'll do if you don't let me come. I don't have anywhere else to go, and I can't bear to stay here. Not another minute. Shayla, I'm desperate. Please. Please let me come."

It would have been useless to try to explain her need for privacy, for some time to herself. She knew that as well as she knew her own name. No one at home believed in her writing, in her book, in her dreams.

Ian's hand alighted on her arm. She glanced over at him, saw the concern in his gaze, gave her head a slight shake, then closed her eyes. Fear nearly strangled her. What about Ian? They were just beginning to—

"Shayla, are you listening to me? I'm desperate. Please. You've got to let me come."

"All right, Anne," she answered at last. "You can

come, if you really need to. Think about it overnight and call me again in the morning.''

"Thanks. I knew I could count on you. And I won't change my mind, but I'll call you in the morning like you want.''

They each said goodbye, then Shayla hung up the phone.

"What is it?'' Ian asked gently.

"Nothing. One of my sisters is coming for a visit. That's all.''

He pulled her into his arms, pressing her cheek against his chest. "I'm here for you, Shayla,'' he whispered.

She swallowed the tears that burned the back of her throat and wondered how long he would be there for her once he laid eyes on her beautiful sister Anne.

Chapter Ten

Frustration was building inside Ian so fast, he thought he might explode from it.

His dinner date with Shayla had gone well. He'd expected things would only get better between them afterward. He was certain she felt *something* for him. The way she'd returned his kisses should've been proof enough of that.

But things had sure gone awry. She'd been avoiding him again, using one excuse after another all week, whether he called or dropped by. She had to work on her book or she had to run errands or she had to take her clothes to the Laundromat. She might as well have said she would rather wash her hair than go out with him again.

Now she'd driven down to Boise in that clunker of a car of hers to pick up her sister, and she hadn't even bothered to inform him of her plans. He'd learned about it from Ty as they rode out that morning to drive cattle from the south range up to Sundance Meadows.

About the tenth time Ian snarled an order at Ty, the young cowboy had had enough.

"If you've got a burr under your saddle 'cause of that gal, Ian, that's your own problem. But I'm not gonna suffer for it."

Ian scowled. What he wouldn't give to punch something! And he just might start with this young ranch hand, good friend or no.

"Man alive," Ty continued, "I've never seen a fella whose saddle was slippin' as fast as yours."

Ian reined in his gelding while muttering a few choice words under his breath.

Ty had the audacity to chuckle before saying, "Why don't you just ask her to marry you and be done with it?"

"We haven't known each other all that long. We've only had one date."

"And that has much to do with anything?" Ty slapped his lariat against his thigh, then whistled for Coira to head off a heifer determined to go back the way they'd come. "You know my folks were married one month to the day after they met? Been together nearly thirty years now."

"It doesn't always work out that way."

"Shoot! As many marriages end in divorce as make it, and I bet plenty of those divorces were between people who knew each other for years before they tied the knot."

Ian remembered Joanne the day she'd driven away from the ranch, and he knew Ty was right. He and Joanne had grown up together, but their marriage had been failing. If she hadn't died in that accident, he was certain she'd have divorced him before long.

"You gonna let Shayla get away from you, boss? You're a fool if you do."

He clenched his jaw, gritting his teeth, refusing to answer.

"Sometimes you're dumber'n a stump, O'Connell."

He was afraid his ranch hand just might have a point.

Despite her misgivings, Shayla had to admit it was wonderful to see her sister.

After meeting Anne at the Boise airport, the two had lunch together. Anne quickly brought Shayla up to date on all the family news, but she circumvented Shayla's inquiries into what horrible thing had sent her running from Portland.

"I don't want to talk about it," was all she would say.

By two o'clock, they were driving north on Highway 55, headed for Rainbow Valley. Anne kept up a steady stream of family gossip until they were past the tiny town of Horseshoe Bend. Then she said, "Now tell me about you, sister dear. What have you been doing with all your leisure time? Imagine, not having to have a job at your age."

Shayla winced. It took enormous control not to reply in anger.

"I haven't had any leisure time," she said slowly, enunciating each word with care. "I've been working hard ever since I got here."

"Oh, that's right." Anne stared out the car window at the passing scenery. "Mom said you were cleaning houses. Why would you want to do that?"

"I was talking about my writing. And I'm not cleaning *houses*. Just one house. A neighboring rancher.'' She pictured Ian in her mind, sitting astride his dappled-gray horse, looking so handsome, so virile. ''And I'm doing it because I need the money. I need to get the cabin in better shape before winter comes. I don't want to freeze to death while I'm writing my book.'' *My book. Remember my book, Anne?*

''But I thought Aunt Lauretta left you money as well as the cabin. Isn't that what Mom and Dad told us?''

''She did, but not enough to see me through.''

Anne sighed dramatically. ''There's never enough money, is there? Thank goodness Mom was willing to buy me an airline ticket or I never could have come to stay with you.''

Thanks a lot, Mom.

''Well, you can't be cleaning house all the time. What about men? Are there any great-looking guys around?''

Again Shayla imagined Ian. ''Yes,'' she answered softly. ''There are.''

''Good. It'll serve Wes right if I find somebody else while I'm here.''

So. It *was* a man who'd sent Anne running to Idaho. Shayla had suspected as much. Her sister changed her boyfriends almost as often as she changed her clothes. Their dad had once suggested installing a revolving front door to make it easier for the boys to come and go in a hurry.

Anne was sure to zero in on Ian the second she saw him. And who could blame her? There were a hundred— no, a thousand!—reasons why any woman would be attracted to Ian O'Connell.

She glanced quickly toward her sister, and her heart sank. Then, as her gaze returned to the road, she silently scolded herself. What would it matter if Ian turned his attentions to Anne? She hadn't been seriously interested in him anyway. Not really. A nice diversion maybe. After all, he was a great kisser. But she wasn't interested in a brief affair, and she definitely didn't want anything more lasting. She wanted a career as a writer. To achieve it would take concentration and hard work.

Maybe it was even a good thing that her sister had come for a visit. Ian could occupy Anne's time and vice versa, which would serve to give Shayla more time to write without interruptions.

Yes, indeed. This was a good thing. Of course it was. So why didn't her foolish heart agree with her head?

The gelding shifted restlessly beneath Ian as he maintained vigil from a clearing on the mountainside.

"Easy, Blue," he murmured. "There's her car now."

He watched as Shayla turned off the dirt road and into her drive, disappearing from view behind the trees.

Sounds carried easily through the forest so Ian knew the instant the engine died. Moments later, the car doors closed, first one, then another. Next he heard Shayla's laughter, a sound that could wrap itself around his heart, followed by their voices, both women talking at once. But he was too far away to hear what they said.

Impatiently he waited what he hoped was an appropriate amount of time, then he nudged Blue with his heels and started down the trail toward the cabin. He rode up the driveway just as a young woman—she had to be Shayla's sister—closed the trunk, then picked up two suitcases, one in each hand. She turned and saw him as he reined in. Her eyes widened a fraction, then she smiled.

"Afternoon." He bent his hat brim. "You must be Anne."

Her smile brightened even more. "Yes. And who are you?"

"Ian O'Connell." He glanced toward the cabin in time to see Shayla step onto the deck. "Glad to see you made it back all right." He swung down from the saddle. Leaving the reins trailing on the ground, he walked over to Anne. "Let me carry those for you."

"Thanks. That's very kind." She handed him the baggage.

With his head, he motioned for her to proceed, then he followed behind her.

Anne Vincent was beautiful, tall and slender with a glorious head of straight, dark hair. She moved with a kind of assurance that was rare in a woman so young. But as attractive as she was, Ian only had eyes for her older sister.

His gaze met with Shayla's. He smiled at her, thinking how glad he was that she was back, safe and sound, wishing he could take her in his arms and keep her there forever.

She didn't return the smile.

Anne stopped beside Shayla, forcing Ian to stop, as well. He was tempted to lean forward and kiss Shayla's cheek.

Before he could act on that impulse, she said, "Anne, this is my neighbor, Ian O'Connell. Ian, my sister, Anne."

"We introduced ourselves already," Anne said, smiling at him again.

Shayla turned and led the way inside. "Anne will be sleeping in the loft. Would you mind carrying her things upstairs?"

"Glad to," he answered.

Anne followed him up the stairs. "So which place is yours, Mr. O'Connell?"

"Just call me Ian." He set the suitcases on the foot of the bed. "I own the ranch across the road." He pointed in the general direction of Paradise.

Her eyes widened. "That huge log house is yours? The one I could see from the highway?"

He nodded.

"I'm impressed."

Anne was pretty, and she knew it, too. Ian could tell by the way she looked at him through thick eyelashes; the way she stood just so, as if posing for a camera; the way she gestured dramatically with her hands. She was used to getting her way with men, to having them fall at her feet in adoration.

Ian had no intention of becoming one of the worshiping masses. He'd already found the woman he wanted, one he found infinitely more desirable.

With a polite nod toward Anne, he exited the loft bedroom and descended the stairs. He found Shayla standing near her computer, staring at the blank screen, her expression wistful.

"Shayla," Anne said from behind Ian. "Shouldn't we ask Mr. O'Connell to stay for supper? He's been so thoughtful to carry in my heavy bags."

Shayla looked up, met his gaze. After a moment's hesitation, she said, "Of course. If he wants to join us."

"I'd love to. But I have a better idea." He smiled at her. "How about if I take the two of you into town. The diner's not fancy, but it's got decent food."

"Oh, I don't know. Perhaps we'd better—"

"You spent almost all day driving to and from Boise," he interrupted. "You shouldn't have to cook, too."

At last Shayla's mouth curved with just a hint of a smile. "If you're sure, Ian, I guess we—"

Anne interrupted this time. "He's sure." She stepped up beside him. "We'd love to go eat with you. Just give me a few minutes to freshen up." She looked at Shayla. "Which way to the bathroom?"

"First door." Shayla pointed toward the short hallway.

As soon as Anne disappeared, Ian moved toward Shayla. "Your sister seems nice."

"She is."

"Mighty young."

"She's twenty-one."

He chuckled. "Like I said, she's mighty young."

"Young, pretty and between boyfriends."

With sudden insight, he realized she expected him to redirect his attentions toward her sister. "Listen, I've got to get Blue back to the ranch. I'll come for you and Anne in about thirty, maybe forty-five minutes. Okay?"

"Okay."

Again he thought about kissing her, and again decided to wait. He didn't want to be interrupted by Anne's reappearance. Besides, he had a plan.

"This is *it?*" Anne leaned forward on the truck seat. "This is the *whole* town?"

"Yup," Ian answered. "Quaint, isn't it?"

Shayla stared out the window, feeling miserable and out of place. When Ian came for them a short while before, Anne had finessed her way into the pickup first, putting herself between Ian and Shayla. She'd done it in such a way that it hadn't looked intentional, but Shayla knew otherwise. Still, Ian hadn't seemed to mind. He'd smiled and chatted with Anne all the way into town.

Shayla felt invisible.

"Here we are," Ian announced as he turned his truck into the diner's parking lot. "It doesn't look like much, but you'll get plenty to eat." He parked the truck, opened his door and stepped out.

"Wait," Anne said before he could close the door. "I'll just slide out your side." She held out her hand in an invitation for him to take hold and assist her out of the vehicle.

Which is what he did.

Shayla wished for a hole in the ground that she could drop through. Or maybe she wanted her sister to fall through that proverbial hole instead.

Ian came around to the passenger side and opened the door for her, offering her a hand down. Reluctantly she accepted the offer, feeling awkward and unattractive.

She was a bit surprised when he didn't release her hand immediately. Instead, he tucked it into the crook of his arm and kept it there by placing his other hand over the top of it. She glanced up and found him smiling at her, a tender smile that took her breath away.

She wished…

If wishes were horses, she could almost hear her mother saying, *then beggars would ride.*

Another vehicle pulled into the parking lot. Ian looked away from Shayla, and his smile broadened. "Ah, good. Ty's right on time."

He'd thoughtfully made it a foursome, brought someone for her to talk with while he and Anne…

She swallowed hard, feeling wretchedly close to tears. By the time she'd blinked them away and was in control of her emotions again, Ty had joined them. Ian made the necessary introductions. Then they went inside the diner.

Somehow she endured the next hour and a half. She participated little in the conversation, only partially aware of the stories Anne, Ty and Ian shared, never quite joining in their frequent laughter. It was so obvious to her that both men were smitten with Anne. And why wouldn't they be? She was everything Shayla was not.

She reminded herself that she should be thankful. Anne would undoubtedly get the full court press from both Ty and Ian now. Which would mean Anne would be gone even more of the time. Shayla would have the solitude she craved. Only a few hours before, she'd been fretting about losing her privacy while Anne stayed with her. Now she would have plenty of it.

Yes, she should be thankful rather than miserable. She should be thankful rather than feeling sorry for herself and wishing for things that could never be.

A disgusting trait, feeling sorry for oneself, she thought as the four of them left the diner.

She was halfway to Ian's truck before she realized Anne wasn't with them. She stopped and looked behind her in time to see her sister sliding into Ty's Jeep, her pretty face wreathed in a smile.

"Don't worry," Ian said near her ear. "I told him to have her home no later than eleven."

"But—"

"I was sort of hoping we'd have some time to ourselves. Just you and me. I figure those moments will be harder to come by while Anne's here."

"You—"

He silenced her by brushing his lips against her forehead while placing his arm around her back. "Come on. Let's go somewhere less public so I can kiss you properly."

Kiss me? She glanced over her shoulder again, watching as Ty's Jeep pulled out of the lot and onto Main Street.

"She's a nice girl, Shayla," Ian said. "But she isn't you."

She's a nice girl, Shayla. But she isn't you.

Lying in bed the next morning, Shayla replayed Ian's words over and over again in her head. She remembered the way he'd held and kissed her as they'd sat on the deck swing. They'd talked a little, looked at the starry night a little. Mostly they'd explored the feel and taste of each other.

It had been a most perfect evening. Better than any other in her life. Ian had made her feel beautiful, special, desirable, important. No one had ever made her feel those things before.

Maybe...just maybe...

Pulling the blankets up to her chin, she wondered what she meant by *maybe*. What was it she wanted from Ian? He'd told her that he wasn't looking for a love affair. He wanted something more permanent, more lasting.

Did *she?*

"What do I want?" she whispered.

She wanted to be a writer. She wanted to be a published novelist. She wanted to create hugely successful mysteries and be interviewed by talk show hosts.

But did that mean she couldn't fall in love? Did it mean she couldn't have a man in her life, too? Did it mean she couldn't have Ian? Weren't many successful writers happily married?

Married?

She groaned as she pulled the blankets over her face. She was jumping the gun. So okay, Ian was attracted to her, but that didn't mean this relationship was bound for more than a few enjoyable evenings of hugging and kissing. She was blowing it all out of proportion. Certainly he hadn't mentioned the word *marriage*. Good grief! She'd suspected Ian was still mourning the death of his wife. Did she want to be a stand-in for Joanne O'Connell? Not on her life.

She heard a door close, followed moments later by the sound of running water. Anne was up, and now Shayla would have to wait a good hour for her chance to use the shower. Of all her sisters, Anne was the worst at hogging the bathroom.

She tossed off the blankets and looked up at the ceiling, saying loudly, "When will I ever learn?"

She got out of bed, pulled on her robe and walked out to the kitchen to put the coffee on. She would need several cups if she hoped to stay awake during this Sunday morning's sermon. She hadn't enjoyed a particularly restful night.

Ian stared at his reflection in the bathroom mirror, his vision blurred, his muscles aching. He couldn't remember the last time he'd had as much trouble falling asleep as he'd had last night.

Leaving Shayla the previous evening had been almost an impossibility. He would have willingly spent the night on the swing, holding her, kissing her, loving her.

Yeah, it was true. He loved her. He loved those baggy T-shirts and old cutoffs she wore. He loved her unruly curls. He loved her slightly turned-up button nose and her soft, pliant lips. He loved her petite height and her generous curves. He loved the way she laughed. He loved how she talked about her brothers and sisters, even when she was confessing her irritation with them. He loved her dedication, her stubbornness, her willingness to try new things.

So what was he going to do about it?

Ty thought Ian should propose, and to heck with knowing each other longer than a few short weeks. Maybe the young cowboy was right. Maybe he should ask her to marry him.

She sure had felt good in his arms last night, soft in all the right places. She'd had his blood running hotter than water in the thermal hot springs that abounded in the area.

He glanced down at the bathroom counter. A can of shaving cream and his razor. Toothpaste and toothbrush. An empty dispenser for three-ounce paper cups. That was it. That was everything on the counter.

He'd seen Shayla's bathroom. Stuff everywhere.

Would he really want—

He grinned at himself in the mirror, interrupting his own silent question. Darn right he would! He'd give her whatever space she needed. It would be worth it to have her close by, day in and day out.

Now all he had to do was convince her it was what she wanted, too.

Chapter Eleven

*C*het looked around the room, feeling desperation well-ing in his chest. The killer had been there. He'd taken True.

First Neal.

Then the sheriff.

And now True.

If she was dead…

No, he wouldn't let himself think that way. She meant too much to him now. In recent weeks he'd discovered there was lots more to True Barry than most people realized. Her tough-gal persona was just that. A per-sona. Beneath that crusty shell beat a sentimental heart of pure gold.

"If you harm one hair on her head," he muttered, "you won't live long enough to regret it." Trouble was, he didn't know who he was threatening.

But True was no dumb bimbo, as he used to think. If

she'd had any time at all before she was taken, she would have left him a clue to the killer's identity or where he had taken her. She wouldn't have gone quietly.

She had to have had time. She had to have left some clue for him. Maybe it was just wishful thinking on his part, but he had to hang on to hope. It was all he had at the moment.

"Hold on, True. Don't give up on me. I'll find you. I swear it."

Peals of laughter broke into Shayla's concentration. Which was just as well, she thought as she rolled her chair backward. She'd never written such tripe.

"Would you like some lunch?" she heard Anne ask.

But her sister wasn't speaking to her. Ty had dropped by. Again.

Shayla rose from her chair and walked toward the front door. The couple was seated on the top step of the deck. Ty's horse grazed in the shade of a nearby aspen.

"How soon do you have to get back to work?" Anne asked him. "It'll only take me a few minutes to whip up a couple of sandwiches and heat some soup."

"I reckon I got time enough."

Shayla pushed open the screen door. "Ty's always got enough time to eat. Don't you, Ty?"

He looked over his shoulder. A sheepish grin served as his affirmative reply. It would have been useless for him to try to deny it. He'd stayed for both meals on Sunday.

Before Shayla could say anything else, she heard the sound of cantering hooves and looked to see Ian riding Blue up the drive. Her heart did its usual flutter at the sight of him. He'd spent yesterday afternoon over here, too.

"Oh, good," Anne said as she rose from the step. "It's a foursome. I'll make extra sandwiches." She hurried inside.

Ty stood. "I'll just give her a hand." He followed Anne into the cabin.

Ian brought Blue to a halt. "I thought I'd find Ty over here." He dismounted, then looked up at her from beneath the brim of his hat. "Glad he is. Gave me an excuse to come see you in the middle of a workday."

Her pulse tripped, then speeded up.

"How's the writing going?" he asked as he climbed the steps toward her.

She shrugged. "So-so."

"Must be tough with people around all the time."

"A little."

"Sorry for intruding."

Her mouth was dry, her head in a dither. She wondered if this was how True felt whenever Chet was around. And would Ian be as upset if *she* were suddenly missing?

"Want me to tell Ty to steer clear of here during the weekdays?"

She gave her head a slight shake. "No. Anne likes his company. And besides, it gives her something to do." She smiled faintly. "I don't think she expected Rainbow to have so few diversions."

"How about if I ask her to do my housekeeping? You could write while she's over at Paradise."

A stinging suspicion pierced her thoughts. Was he looking for a way to be alone with Anne?

He touched her cheek with his fingertips. "It's okay to think about your own needs once in a while, Shayla."

Oh, cowboy, she thought as she met his gaze, *you have no idea how much I'm thinking about my own needs.*

A slow smile curved his mouth, and a flicker of something in his coffee-brown eyes told her she was wrong. He *did* know.

"Maybe I should see if Anne needs help," she said, taking a step backward.

He stopped her with a hand on her arm. "Ty's already helping her."

"Well, I should—"

"Join me on the swing," he finished for her, his grin broadening. Then he added, "Besides, I came to ask you something."

She could have told him he'd be wasting his time, asking her anything. She hadn't been thinking straight. Not for two days. Not since she'd lain awake the better share of the night and found herself thinking words like *love* and *marriage*.

"I've got to drive down to Boise tomorrow," he said as they settled onto the swing. "Leigh and Jim are flying in with the twins. I'll be staying overnight, then coming back the next day after they fly out again. I thought you might like to come along. You could meet my sister and her husband."

He wanted her to meet his family? That sounded serious.

"'Course, I don't know how much fun it'll be driving back with two six-year-old girls. I'm no expert with kids like you are. Guess that'd be another good reason for you to come along, wouldn't it?"

It took a few seconds for that comment to sink in. When it did, she asked, "The twins are coming back with you?"

"I was sure I'd already told you." He pushed his hat back on his head, then scratched his temple. "But I'm not surprised if I forgot to mention it. Whenever I'm with you, I'm lucky if I can remember my own name.'' He gave her a slow, lazy kind of smile before continuing. ''Leigh and Jim are going overseas for his job, and they're leaving their girls in my care.''

He wanted help with his nieces. He thought her an expert with kids. It wasn't that he was interested in her. Not really.

''How about it, Shayla?''

She felt stiff and cold inside. ''I don't think so. Anne's here and—''

''Ty'll keep your sister busy while you're gone. She'll never even—''

''No.'' She stood up. ''I prefer not to go. But thanks for asking. Excuse me. I...I've got something I must do inside.'' She hurried away before she could burst into tears of disappointment in front of him.

She'd thought...

She'd hoped...

But she should have known better.

''What did I say?'' Ian asked himself as the screen door swung closed behind Shayla. He knew he'd upset her. But for the life of him, he didn't know why.

Just as he stood up, Anne came through the doorway. ''What happened?''

''I don't know.''

''Well, you must have done *something*. Shayla never cries. She's always been the strongest one in the family.''

''She's crying?'' He moved forward. ''I'd better try to apologize.''

Anne blocked the entrance with her body. ''She said she was going to lie down.'' She stared at him with a suspicious gaze.

"All I did was ask her to go with me to Boise. I wanted her to meet my sister and her husband."

"I guess she doesn't want to go."

"Anne, listen. I—"

She put her hand on his chest, keeping him outside. "Nobody hurts my big sister, Mr. O'Connell."

"But I didn't mean to."

"I think you'd better go."

He wanted to argue with her. He wanted to push his way past her and go after Shayla. But he had the feeling Anne would light into him like an angry cat, claws bared, if he did.

He took a step away from the door. "All right. But tell her I'll come see her as soon as I get back. Tell her that I'm sorry for...for whatever I said wrong."

Anne remained dubious, judging by her expression and the set of her shoulders.

Women!

Ian turned and descended the steps.

When could a man ever figure a woman out? One minute, some poor slob thought he was getting along perfectly with his favorite gal, and then, *wham!* Everything was screwed up between them.

Ian was still mumbling the same sort of sentiments the next day during the drive to Boise. He kept trying to figure out what it was he'd said or done to upset Shayla as he waited for the airplane carrying the Parker family. But try as he might, he found no answers.

He'd offered to let Anne work for him so Shayla would have time alone to write. He'd invited her to come to Boise to meet Leigh and Jim. He'd admitted that being around her made him forget his own name. None of those things should have upset her. So what had? What had he done or said to make her cry, to make her hide from him?

Passengers began to pour out of Arrivals, intruding on his troubled musings. For now, he'd have to pay attention to his sister and her family. But as soon as he got back to Rainbow Valley, he was going to get some answers.

"Ian!"

He grinned as his gaze met with his sister's over the heads of other passengers. "Hey, Leigh!" He waved. "Jim!"

Moments later, he was hugging Leigh and shaking his brother-in-law's hand. Then he was reintroduced to Cathy and Angie, a pair of dark-haired angels if ever he'd seen any.

"Hi, Uncle Ian," they said in unison, their smiles shy, their eyes slightly downcast.

"Hi, yourself. Wow! I'd forgotten how identical you are. How can I tell you apart?"

Their smiles grew.

"Nobody can," one of them said.

"Except Mommy and Daddy," the other added.

A smart man would have known right then that he was in trouble.

Ian didn't have a clue.

He put his arm around Leigh's shoulders. "It's great to see you, sis. How's Mom?" They started down the corridor.

"She's fine. The new medication she's on has helped ease that pain in her hip." She glanced at him as they walked. "She's got a steady beau."

"You're kidding."

"Nope. And I think it's getting serious."

Ian released a soft whistle. "Mom with a boyfriend. Isn't that something?"

"How about you?" She gently jabbed him in the ribs. "Anybody special in your life?"

He hesitated, then answered, "As a matter of fact, yes."

It must have been something in his voice that caused Leigh to stop, forcing him to do the same. She looked up at him for several moments. "Well, I'll be. Ian, you're in love, aren't you?"

He shrugged first. Then he nodded. "But I'm not sure what she feels for me," he said quickly before Leigh could ask that particular question. "One moment I think there's hope. The next..." He let his voice trail into silence as he shrugged again.

"Who is she? Do I know her?"

"No." They started walking again. "She's fairly new to the valley."

"Your neighbor. The housekeeper. I *knew* it!"

"She's not a housekeeper. She's a writer. She's working on a mystery novel right now. Her name's Shayla Vincent. She's old Mrs. Erickson's great-niece."

"I'm happy for you, Ian. I hope it works out." She tightened her arm around his waist. "I wish I could have met her before leaving the country."

"Me, too," he said softly, remembering the scene on Shayla's deck and wishing he knew what had gone wrong.

True could escape from the murderous Mitchell Jones. Then she could sneak up on Chet and strangle him while he was sleeping. Or maybe she could put some horrible drug in his coffee when he came in to eat at the diner. She could watch him die a miserable, painful death, writhing in agony on the floor, begging for mercy, which she most certainly would not give. Or there was always Chinese water torture or bamboo shoots beneath the fingernails.

There had to be a hundred different ways True Barry could make Chet Morrison suffer.

"I wish you'd tell me what it was Ian did," Anne said, her voice laced with concern.

Shayla looked up from the manuscript pages she was supposed to be revising. "What?"

"What did he do?"

She shook her head. "It isn't important."

"It must be or you wouldn't be moping."

"I'm not moping. I'm *trying*—" she gave her sister a pointed look "—to get some work done."

"Well, I like Ian, and so do you, whether you want to admit it or not." Anne flopped down onto the sofa across from Shayla and stretched out her long legs, crossing one ankle over the other. She tucked her hands behind her head. "You should have seen his face. He couldn't imagine what he'd said to upset you. Whatever it was, he regrets it. You ought to give him the benefit of the doubt."

Shayla released a deep sigh. "Leave it alone, Anne."

"You don't just like him, you know. You're in love with him."

"I most certainly am not." She dropped the manuscript pages onto the rickety coffee table and got up from her chair. "Now let's change the subject."

"To what?" Anne raised one leg and stared at her toenails. "I need to fix my polish," she said. "Do you have any polish remover down here?"

"No!" Shayla snapped.

"Well, you don't have to bite my head off. *I* didn't do anything."

"Ooh!" Shayla headed out of the cabin, letting the screen door slam behind her. She almost flew down the steps, then headed up the hillside that rose behind the cabin. She needed to get far away so she could scream without anybody hearing her.

She'd walked for a good five minutes before she realized that the sound she heard was Honey Girl's familiar yap. She stopped and turned. Sure enough, there was the puppy, struggling to catch up with her.

"How did you get out of the house?" she asked as she knelt down.

Honey Girl scampered through the underbrush, undaunted and determined to reach her mistress.

"Anne let you out, didn't she?"

The puppy barked, as if saying, "Yes!"

"That was a rotten thing for her to do."

As she lifted Honey Girl into her arms, she looked down the mountain toward the cabin. Anne stood at the corner of the deck, staring up the hillside, shading her eyes with one hand.

"That was a rotten thing to do!" Shayla shouted.

Her sister simply raised a hand in a wave, then retreated indoors.

"I don't love him," she said aloud to the puppy. "I don't. He's handsome, and he's interesting." She continued walking, holding Honey Girl against her chest. "And he does make me go all warm and soft inside when he kisses me. But that's just sexual attraction. It doesn't have anything to do with love."

Dried leaves and old pine needles crunched beneath her feet. The puppy licked Shayla's chin.

"Okay, you're right. He is actually quite nice, and it

was kind of him to give you to me and to teach me to ride.''

The sun beat warm upon her back.

''But I'm not about to become a nursemaid for his nieces. I went through that with Gordon. I'm not going through it again. He just wants an expert with kids. An expert. Bah!'' She kicked at the ground with the toe of her shoe. ''Expert *this,* Ian O'Connell.''

Honey Girl wiggled and whined, begging down.

Shayla obliged the puppy. ''I hope those kids drive your former master crazy. It would serve him right. I helped raise my brothers and sisters. I don't want to help raise anybody else's kids. Not even temporarily. I don't want to be the expert on kids.'' She looked up at the blue sky and raised her voice to shout, ''I want to be a writer!''

But no one heard her.

No one ever heard her.

Or so it seemed.

Angie started crying at the airport the next morning. Or was it Cathy who was in tears? Ian wasn't certain. He couldn't tell them apart, even when Leigh dressed them differently.

''I don't wanna stay with Uncle Ian. I wanna go with you and Daddy.''

''You can't, sweetheart,'' Leigh said, smoothing back her daughter's hair. ''We've talked about this.''

The other twin started crying, too. ''Why couldn't we stay with Gramma? I want my own room.''

''Your grandmother doesn't have the energy to keep you for so long.'' Leigh glanced at Jim for help.

''Listen,'' their dad offered. ''Remember how we told you your uncle Ian has horses and dogs and cows and all sorts of neat things on the ranch. You'll get to go swimming and riding. It'll be like going to camp."

The final boarding announcement blared over the loudspeaker.

"I'm afraid of horses," one of the girls cried.

"We've got to go." Leigh gave each of her daughters a tight hug and a kiss on the cheek. "Be good for your uncle Ian. We'll call just as soon as we can." She was crying now, too.

"Mommy, don't go. Daddy!"

Leigh and Jim disengaged themselves as gently as they could, but Ian still had to hold the twins to keep them from following their parents down the ramp.

The crying and wailing kept up as the last passengers boarded, as the ground crew moved the boarding ramp away from the plane, as the aircraft was pushed back from the terminal, and right up until the plane taxied out to the runway and took off. In fact, Ian was beginning to believe the two girls would never stop crying.

Give him a bucking bronco any day of the week, he thought as he stared helplessly at the whimpering children who were now clinging to each other as if their lives depended upon it. He sure could have used Shayla right about now. She would have known how to talk to the twins, how to make them feel better.

He cleared his throat. "It's time we head for the ranch. It's getting late and we've got a long drive."

"I don't want to go with you," one of them answered, stomping her foot and glaring at him with defiant eyes.

"You don't have any choice." He forced himself to be calm.

"You can't make us go," the other one retorted.

His temper was beginning to fray. "I'm afraid you're wrong about that, little girl."

"I'm Cathy. You don't even know my name."

"Sorry. Like I said yesterday, I can't tell you apart."

"Mommy can," Angie cried.

"She never mixes us up," Cathy interjected.

He wondered what the penalty was for deserting two six-year-olds in an airport. Or maybe, he thought in desperation, he should just tell someone that these girls' parents had left them there unattended, with no one to care for them. They might have to turn the plane around.

"I wanna go home. I want my mommy."

Oh, help! he silently prayed.

He grabbed the twins, each by a hand, and headed out of the terminal, all the time expecting someone to have him arrested for abducting children.

That's almost what happened.

Ian was awakened at three in the morning by loud knocking on his front door. He hadn't fallen asleep until well after midnight, so it took him a few moments to orient himself. Then he sleepily shuffled and stumbled his way downstairs.

This had better be important, he silently groused. If not, he'd strangle whoever was on the other side of that door. Especially if the twins woke up because of it.

He stubbed his toe on the door as he yanked it open, serving to increase his foul mood.

"What is it?" He stopped abruptly, blinked against the bright headlights shining in his face. "Sheriff?" Anger was replaced by alarm. The last time an officer of the law had arrived on his front porch unexpectedly, it was with the news of Joanne's death.

Sheriff Paul Adamson pushed his hat up his forehead with his thumb. "Sorry to bother you in the middle of the night, Ian, but we got a call."

"A call?" He glanced toward the car again. A deputy was standing beside the open passenger door. "What call?"

"You got some girls here. Little girls. Maybe five or six years old?"

Alarm turned to outright fear. Had the plane gone down? Were Jim and Leigh—

"You mind if I come in?" the sheriff asked, his voice suddenly gruff.

He didn't move. "Is it Jim and Leigh? Was there a plane crash?"

"Just answer my question, Ian. You got two little girls inside your house?"

"Yes. My nieces. Is this about their parents? If something's happened to my sister, just tell me now."

Paul removed his hat. "Maybe you'd better let me come inside. And nothing's happened to Leigh that I'm aware of."

Ian opened the door wider with one hand while running the fingers of his other hand through his hair. He was confused, tired and cranky. If it wasn't because of bad news, just what *had* brought Sheriff Adamson to his doorstep at 3:00 a.m.?

"About your nieces…" Paul began after stepping into the entry. "I need to see them."

"What for? It's the middle of the night. They're asleep."

"Well, seems they called 9-1-1. Something about being taken from their parents."

Ian's gaze darted toward the stairs. "Why those little…" He couldn't finish the sentence. He could hardly think straight. They'd called the cops on him!

"That's sorta what I figured," Paul said, the gruffness

absent now, replaced by a hint of amusement. "But I still need to see them."

Without a word, Ian headed up the stairs and down the hall to the guest bedroom. He pushed open the door and flicked on the light switch. Cathy and Angie sat in the middle of the bed, hugging one another and staring at him, wide-eyed and innocent looking.

Innocent? *Ha!* A more terrible twosome he'd never encountered.

"Here they are, Sheriff."

Paul followed him into the bedroom, removing his hat as he did so. "Did one of you little ladies dial 9-1-1?"

They both started to cry at once. Whatever reply they tried to make was garbled with tears of woe.

Thirty minutes later, with matters finally straightened out, Ian saw the sheriff to the front door.

"Don't be too hard on 'em," Paul said with a chuckle. "They're just homesick for their mom and dad."

Ian nodded but didn't speak. He was kind of sick himself. Taking care of the twins wasn't going to be the fun and games he'd hoped it would be.

He was in trouble.

Big trouble.

Chapter Twelve

By Friday, Shayla knew she couldn't avoid her duties at Paradise another day. She'd made an agreement with Ian. He'd already kept his part of the bargain, making repairs to her roof and other things around the cabin. She had to make certain his house was kept clean. And with two children living there now, it had to be somewhat chaotic.

Besides, curiosity was getting the better of her. She hadn't seen him since before his return two days ago with his nieces. Anne was no help; she hadn't mentioned Ian's name all week, although Shayla was certain her sister and the almost-ever-present Ty had discussed him when they were out of her hearing.

Of course, nothing could have compelled her to *ask* Anne what she knew.

As she drove up to the ranch house shortly after one o'clock in the afternoon, she saw Ty and Mick riding away from the barn at a full gallop. She pulled the car into her now-customary spot in the shade of a tree outside the back entrance to the house. When she shut off the engine, she knew why the cowboys had been in full retreat. It sounded like a reenactment of the Battle of the Little Big Horn was taking place inside.

"I won't! I won't!" two voices shrieked in unison.

"Yes, you will!" That was Ian shouting.

She entered through the open doorway, pausing in the mudroom to view the scene beyond.

Two little girls, dark hair in uneven ponytails, sat at the table. Plates of untouched food were in front of them. Ian stood in the center of the kitchen, glaring at the children, his backside against the island, his arms crossed over his chest.

"You *are* going to eat your vegetables," he said, speaking slowly and deliberately.

"You can't make us," one of the girls retorted.

Ian's neck and the tops of his ears turned bright red, and for a moment, Shayla thought his eyes might bulge right out of their sockets.

Poor man. He was hanging on to his temper by a thread. Despite herself, she felt sorry for him.

"Excuse me," she interjected into the tense silence. "Have I come at a bad time?"

He turned toward her with a look of sheer desperation. "Shayla!"

"Who're you?" one of the twins demanded suspiciously.

"I'm Shayla Vincent, your uncle's neighbor. I do some housecleaning for him." As she spoke, she moved toward the table. "Let's see. Your uncle told me your names once. Is it Carolyn and Abigail?" Her error was intentional, and it brought the desired results.

"No!" one exclaimed.

"I'm Cathy," the other said. "And she's Angie."

"Ah, yes. Cathy and Angie. Very pretty names."

Shayla studied their faces. Cathy had more freckles across the bridge of her nose. Angie had a cowlick in the center of her dark bangs. And unless she'd totally lost her knack for reading children, these two were trouble with a capital *T* when they weren't getting their way. She also knew they had to be homesick and lonely for their parents.

"They're supposed to be eating their lunch," Ian volunteered from behind her.

Shayla glanced over her shoulder. He didn't look like he'd had much sleep. His eyes were bloodshot.

"They don't like peas," he added.

She turned back to the girls and checked out their untouched plates. "Lasagna is my favorite. Don't you like that, either?"

"It won't be as good as Mommy's," Cathy argued.

It was obvious which twin was the ringleader.

"But you can't know that until you try it." Shayla leaned forward, speaking softly. "Let's find a compromise, shall we? You eat at least some of your lasagna, and I'll talk to your uncle about the peas."

Cathy and Angie exchanged looks, then Cathy answered, "Okay. We'll try it."

"Can you tell me what vegetables you *do* like? Then maybe you and your uncle won't have to go through this again."

"Corn."

"Potatoes."

"And carrots."

"Green beans are okay. Mommy fixes them with bacon."

Shayla nodded as she straightened. "Do you want me to warm up your lasagna in the microwave?"

"Yes, please," they said at the same time.

She took their plates and put them in the microwave. After returning the reheated food to the table, she motioned for Ian to follow her outside, moving away from the door and out of hearing distance.

"Has it been that rough?" she asked.

"You must have heard. It's all over town."

"What's all over town?"

Ian raised an eyebrow. "Anne hasn't told you?"

She shook her head.

"Then you're the *only* person in Rainbow Valley who doesn't know about it." He frowned. "The boys at the hardware store are having a grand old time at my expense."

"About what?"

"They called the sheriff to have me arrested. In the middle of the night, they dialed 9-1-1 and asked for help. They said they'd been kidnaped or something. Can you believe that?"

Shayla was confused. "*Who* did?"

"The six-year-old twin terrors." He did everything but shudder. "And that's only the *first* thing they've done since we got here. It hasn't gotten much better."

She couldn't stop herself from laughing once she understood what he was telling her.

"It isn't funny, Shayla. I thought I'd be this great uncle, and instead they hate me."

Her laughter died instantly. "They don't hate you." She had to resist the urge to hug him. "They just don't know you well enough yet. They're little girls who've been taken from their home and their parents and everything that's familiar. They're lonely and homesick."

"I know. But what do I do about it?"

"For starters, be patient with them." She supposed it wasn't necessary to tell him it could get worse before it got better. She glanced toward the house. "Who's staying with them during the day while you're working?"

"I'm not working. I've been here all the time. Twenty-four hours a day." His frustration was obvious in his tone of voice. "I'd planned to teach them how to ride so they could go with me during the day, but they don't want to learn."

Now wasn't that just like a man? Shayla thought.

"They're children, Ian. Not ranch hands."

"I figured it would be fun for them."

"You can't tell me that Leigh expected you to keep them with you all day long every day. She grew up here. She knows how much work it is."

"Well, no. Of course she didn't." He raked the fingers of one hand through his hair. "She said she would pay for whatever childcare was necessary."

"Then it's time you hired someone."

"Would you help me?" he asked softly. "I don't know anything about hiring a sitter for kids. Especially not *these* little hellions. If you'd just help me with the interviews. Make sure I ask the right questions."

A wave of relief washed over her. She'd been afraid he was going to ask her to be their sitter. She'd been afraid he wouldn't give a thought to how important her writing was to her, just as Anne hadn't when she'd asked to come to Idaho to stay with Shayla.

"Would you?" he repeated.

"Of course." She smiled up at him. "I'd be happy to help."

Maybe her sister was right. Maybe she was falling in love with Ian.

Maybe she already had.

* * *

Ian invited Shayla to stay and eat with the family, and she accepted. With her present, suppertime went better than it had the previous two nights.

After they were done eating, she suggested a game of Chinese checkers. The four of them gathered around the big coffee table in the great room and played for more than an hour. Finally, around eight o'clock, she offered to see to the children's bath and get them ready for bed.

Ian stayed downstairs and did the dishes.

This evening had been perfect, he thought. Exactly what he'd imagined it would be like, having Leigh's twins with him. And it was all because of Shayla. She was wonderful with the girls. She seemed to know exactly how to put them at ease, how to make them feel more at home and less lonely for their parents. She had a way of speaking to them that had them eating out of her hand.

And she could tell them apart. How did she do *that?*

She was amazing, his Shayla.

His Shayla.

He stopped scrubbing the skillet and glanced toward the hall. He could hear her speaking softly, followed by children's laughter.

His Shayla.

He loved her. He wouldn't love her more a month from now or a year from now, because he already loved her with his whole heart.

Tonight. He should ask her tonight to marry him. Before she left he should ask her.

"Ian." As if summoned by his thoughts, Shayla appeared in the kitchen doorway. "They're ready for you to tell them good-night."

He grabbed a dish towel and dried his hands. His mouth was as dry as cotton. He'd been nothing but a kid himself the last time he'd proposed marriage. He wondered if he would have the courage to say the words.

Tossing the towel aside, he followed her out of the kitchen, down the hall, up the stairs and into the bedroom where Cathy and Angie were already tucked into bed. Their hair had been washed, dried and neatly combed. Their faces were scrubbed and shining. They looked almost angelic. It was easy to forget their behavior of the past two days.

He sat on the edge of the bed, leaned over and kissed them each on the cheek. "Good night, Cathy. Good night, Angie."

"I'm Angie. She's Cathy."

"Oh. Sorry." He glanced toward the doorway where Shayla was waiting. "I'll get it right eventually."

She smiled at him. "Sure you will."

Looking at the girls again, he said, "How'd you like to go swimming at the lake tomorrow? We'll make a day of it."

"Yes!" they exclaimed.

Then Cathy said, "Can Shayla come, too?"

"Sure. If she wants." He stood. "Good night. See you in the morning."

Shayla flicked off the light switch.

"Good night, Uncle Ian."

"Good night, Shayla."

"Good night, you two."

As he stepped out of the darkened bedroom, Ian was awash in good feelings. This was how it was supposed to be. This was how it could be with Shayla as his wife.

They were both silent as they went down the stairs,

returning to the kitchen where she retrieved her purse from the counter.

"Leaving already?" He was disappointed. He didn't want the evening to end.

"It's time. I hadn't meant to spend the day here."

Go on. Ask her!

She started toward the back door. He followed.

"Will you join us at the lake tomorrow? The girls want you to come."

She glanced over at him. "I really shouldn't. I'm so far behind."

"You worked a miracle here today. It's the first time they've gone to bed without tears."

They walked to her car. She stopped, turned toward him. "It wasn't anything special."

"You're wrong about that." He drew closer to her. "It was special. *You're* special."

Dusk made it difficult to read what was in her eyes as he caressed her cheek with one hand.

"Shayla, I...I want to apologize for Monday. Whatever I said to hurt you, I didn't mean to."

"I know."

"I guess I've been on my own for too long. Me, the dogs, horses and cattle. A man tends to forget how to word things right. Especially to a woman."

"I overreacted."

"No. Let me say this." Silently he prayed, *And let me say it right.* "You've come to mean a lot to me. I think I've made that pretty clear, the times we've been together. But I don't think you know how much. I don't think *I* knew how much until this past week."

"Ian—"

He rushed to say it before he lost his nerve. "I love you, Shayla. I want to marry you."

"What?"

"I want to marry you. I want you to be my wife, to live with me in this big old house. I want you and me to be a family, to make Paradise a real home. I want us to grow old together, sitting on the front porch in rocking chairs and reminiscing about the past."

Was that the glitter of unshed tears he saw in her eyes as she stared up at him?

"Since the first day I saw you over at your cabin, stabbing the air with that silly knife of yours, you've filled my thoughts. I don't want to be without you."

"I came here to write a book," she whispered.

"You can still write. I would do everything in my power not to get in the way of that dream. I swear to you. Say yes. Say you'll marry me."

For some crazy reason, Shayla believed him. He loved her. He wouldn't get in the way of her dreams.

"I'll take care of you," he said as he drew her into his embrace, pressing her cheek against his chest. "You'd never have to worry about a leaky roof or a chimney that won't draw or anything else."

She closed her eyes. It would be wonderful to have someone take care of her. She'd spent her entire life— or so it seemed—taking care of others, helping her mother, watching her sisters and brothers grow up. Wouldn't it be nice to have someone looking after her for a change? Someone strong like Ian O'Connell?

"Is there a chance you might love me, too?" he asked, his breath warm against the top of her head.

There was more than a chance.

But before she could form a reply, she heard a distant crash, followed by a panicked scream. "Uncle Ian!"

Shayla and Ian broke apart and raised their eyes to an open second-story window.

"Uncle Ian!"

He raced toward the house. Shayla followed right behind him. They found the two girls in Joanne's studio. A bookcase had toppled over. Beside it, surrounded by books, sat Angie, blood running from a wound on her head.

"What happened?" Ian shouted above the girl's cries.

"She got hit on the head," Cathy answered.

Ian had to pry Angie's fingers out of the way to get a look. While he was doing so, Shayla retrieved a towel from the bathroom. She was back in time to see him lifting the child off the floor.

"This needs stitches," he told her. "Can you drive?"

"Of course." She held the towel toward Angie. "Hold this against your head, sweetheart. Go on. Take it. It'll help." She turned toward Angie's frightened twin. "Come on, Cathy. Let's go. It'll be okay."

With hurried steps, they raced outside, Ian carrying the injured child. They piled into Ian's truck. Gravel sprayed up behind the tires as Shayla gunned the engine and peeled out of the drive.

Ian paced the doctor's waiting room. What was taking so long? Dr. Dobbins had said it wasn't anything serious.

He glanced over his shoulder. Shayla was seated on a padded office chair, Cathy in her lap. She stroked the child's back slowly, all the time speaking words of reassurance near her ear. He wouldn't mind a few words of reassurance himself.

She looked up, found him watching her. She offered a gentle smile before saying, "She's okay."

"You read my mind."

"It isn't hard to do." She patted the seat of the chair next to her. "Come over here and sit down."

He glanced back at the doctor's office door, then did as she'd told him.

"Head wounds bleed more than any other," Shayla said. "Just a scratch and it looks like a person will bleed to death before it stops."

"I should have been watching them."

"You can't watch them every minute."

He groaned as he leaned the back of his head against the wall. He stared up at the ceiling. "I don't know what I'd've done if you hadn't been there. We'd better get married soon 'cause I'll never survive these two without you." He released another groan as he closed his eyes.

The office door opened. "Ian," the doctor said.

He was on his feet instantly. "Yes."

"Come inside, please."

"Is she—"

"Angie is just fine. Come in, and we'll talk about it."

"Shayla," Cathy whispered as the door swung closed behind her uncle and the doctor. "Is Angie really gonna be okay?"

Shayla swallowed the lump in her throat, blinked away the hot tears that burned her eyes. "Of course she is. She's going to be fine."

We'd better get married soon 'cause I'll never survive these two without you.

Never had words cut so deeply as those. Not ever.

"It's my fault Angie's hurt." Cathy started to cry again. "I knocked it down. Angie wasn't doin' anything." She buried her face against Shayla's T-shirt. "I wanted to see that doll up on the top shelf, but when I started to climb, it all fell down and—"

"It was an accident, sweetheart. And your sister will be fine in no time."

We'd better get married soon 'cause I'll never survive these two without you.

He hadn't meant it the way it sounded. Deep in her heart, she knew he hadn't meant it that way. But there it was anyway. It stood between them like a yawning canyon. For all his promises that he would support her and never stand in her way, she knew marriage to him would be a mistake. The demands of life and her eagerness to please him would intrude, little by little, until she allowed them to destroy her hopes and dreams.

She couldn't marry him, and she had to tell him so tonight.

"She refused my proposal."

Ty let the latigo drop and looked over the top of the saddle at Ian. "What?"

"You heard me right. I asked her to marry me last night, and she refused."

"But why?"

"She said she isn't ready to get married."

"Doesn't figure." Ty resumed saddling his horse. "I'd've sworn she had a hankerin' for you. Truth is, I told her so to her face a while back. 'Course, Lord only knows why she'd fall in love with the likes of you, but that's what I thought. Still do."

Ian had thought she loved him, too. Right up until the instant they heard Cathy's cry for help, he'd have bet Shayla was going to accept his proposal of marriage. In his mind, the deed had already been done. He'd been ready to start moving her things over to the ranch.

"Never can figure a woman," Ty said. "Contrary creatures. Every last one of 'em."

Ian supposed Ty meant Anne, but he didn't ask. He couldn't bring himself to. He merely mumbled, "Yeah," then turned and left the barn.

He stopped halfway to the house and gazed off in the direction of the cabin. Dang! Why *was* she being so contrary? She *did* love him. He was sure of it. He couldn't be that wrong.

"Can we go now, Uncle Ian?"

He glanced toward the truck. The twins were already in the cab. At least he could tell who had asked the question. Cathy. The one without a bandage on her head.

"Just one second," he called to them, then spun on his heel and strode back to the barn. "Ty? You really think all she's being is contrary?"

His friend chuckled before answering. "Pretty sure, boss." He swung up into the saddle, then saluted Ian. "You and the gals have a good time over in McCall. I'll see what I can find out from Anne."

"Thanks. I appreciate it."

"Sure thing. Glad to help. Besides, if Shayla leaves Rainbow Valley, what's gonna bring her pretty sister back for visits every now and again?"

Ian grinned, feeling a bit more lighthearted than moments before. "Maybe you'll have to do some proposing yourself."

"Not this cowboy. I'm not ready to shorten my stirrups just yet, and neither is Anne. But that doesn't mean we aren't enjoyin' being together now." Ty clucked to his horse and rode off with a wave of farewell.

Not much later, Ian and the girls drove down the highway on their way to McCall and a day at the beach. Traffic was crazy. Every flatlander with a camp trailer seemed to be on the road in front of him, most of them slowing down to ten miles per hour at every curve in the road. This being Idaho, there were plenty of curves.

"How come Shayla didn't come?" Cathy asked.

"She had other things to do."

"I like her," Cathy continued. "She's real nice."

He glanced to his right, then back at the road. "Yeah. I think so, too."

"You and her gonna get married?" This from Angie.

"I was sorta hoping we would," he confessed. "But I'm not sure she feels the same."

Cathy leaned forward on the seat. "We could help. Couldn't we, Angie?"

"Sure!" her twin replied.

Flicking on his left turn signal in preparation for passing another slow-moving vehicle, he muttered, "I could use all the help I can get."

Chapter Thirteen

"**I**'m not taking no for an answer." Anne stood with her feet slightly apart, her knuckles resting on her hips in a Wonder Woman stance. She looked as determined and invincible as that mythical character, too. "You *are* going with us to the picnic and fireworks."

"I don't *feel* like going," Shayla protested.

"Well, tough cookies. You're going whether you feel like it or not. I've listened to all the sighs I can tolerate for one day."

"I've done no such thing."

"The heck you haven't. If your face gets any longer, you're going to have to throw it over your shoulders like the ears of a basset hound."

Shayla swiveled her chair toward her computer screen. "I'm going to stay home and write."

"*You* are a coward, Shayla Vincent. Have some backbone. Show what you're made of. If you don't want anything to do with Ian, then fine. That's your own business. But don't hide out here like some old hermit.''

"Go away."

Anne laughed. Wickedly. "Sister dear, I'm not going anywhere. As Ty would say, 'I'm gonna stick to you like a burr under a saddle.'''

"Oh, ple-e-e-z-e."

"So give up and agree to go with us."

"All right. All right. I'll go. Just leave me alone for the afternoon."

Laughing again, Anne sauntered out of the cabin. A few minutes later, Ty's Jeep engine revved to life, a door closed, and Shayla heard them drive away.

At last. Peace and quiet. Now she could get back to her story.

I love you, Shayla. I want to marry you.

No, she wasn't going to think about Ian. She wasn't going to replay it all again. She'd done little else for the past forty-two hours.

I want us to be a family.

A family. That meant kids. He would want babies. Well, she didn't. She had a career to think about.

I'll take care of you.

She didn't need to be taken care of. She could take care of herself. Oh, she'd suffered a momentary weakness when he'd first said those words, thinking it would be wonderful, but she really wouldn't want such a thing. She was destined to be a woman of the twenty-first century. Independent. Self-sufficient.

Giggles and whispers intruded on her thoughts. She turned quickly toward the sounds to find two little girls peering at her through the screen door. Cathy and Angie.

Her heart skipped a beat. Ian! He'd come to see her.

"Hi," the girls said.

"Whatcha doin'?" Cathy asked.

"Can we come in?" Angie inquired.

Shayla stood and walked to the door, bracing herself for the moment she would see their uncle.

"You weren't in church this morning." Cathy pulled open the screen door. "Uncle Ian was lookin' for you there. He says you don't miss church for no reason."

Angie followed her sister inside. "He feels bad He thinks you didn't go 'cause of him."

Shayla looked outside. "Where *is* your uncle?"

"He fell asleep on the couch right after lunch. He was real tired."

She glanced over her shoulder at the twins. "You mean, he doesn't know you're here?"

Wide-eyed with innocence, Angie answered, "We didn't wanna wake him. He was snoring."

"You walked over here by yourselves?"

A vision of her near-encounter with Satan, the cantankerous old bull, flashed in Shayla's mind. The alternative, that they'd come by way of the highway, wasn't any more comforting. She felt sick to her stomach.

"You two sit down over there while I call your uncle. He'll be worried about you."

"He won't be worried. He's asleep. Remember?"

Shayla ignored whichever twin had spoken and hurried toward the telephone. She dialed the number quickly, then waited through several rings before she heard Ian's drowsy answer.

"Ian. It's Shayla. Did you know that Cathy and Angie are over at my place?"

"What? The twins? Where?"

"They walked over here. *By themselves!*"

That seemed to bring him fully awake.

"I'll be right there." He hung up without another word.

Shayla turned toward the girls, now seated side by side on the sofa. "It was a naughty thing you did. You must not leave the ranch without getting permission from an adult. And I think you already know that."

The twins turned toward one another, exchanged glances, then looked at Shayla again. Their eyes glittered with real tears.

"We didn't mean to do anything wrong," Angie whispered. "We just wanted to see you again."

"Don't you want to see us anymore?" Cathy added, followed by a tiny sob.

She couldn't resist their tears. She went to sit between them on the couch. Placing an arm around each one, she hugged them to her sides.

"Of course I want to see you," she said gently. "But you have to understand. You could have been hurt, coming all this way by yourselves. What if you'd gotten lost on your way here? Your uncle wouldn't have known where to look for you or how to find you."

"We didn't mean to be bad."

"Is Uncle Ian gonna hate us?"

"You aren't bad, but you did make a bad choice. And no, your uncle isn't going to hate you. He loves you very, very much."

Angie buried her face against Shayla's side. "I wish Mommy and Daddy were here."

"Me, too," Cathy choked out between sobs.

Me, too, Shayla thought while giving them each a kiss on the top of their heads.

That's how Ian found them, bunched together on the sofa, the two girls crying and Shayla trying to comfort them. He didn't bother to knock. He just opened the screen door and went in. Shayla heard him first and glanced up.

Like a dying man in the desert, he drank in the sight of her, momentarily forgetting why he'd come.

"Your uncle's here," she said softly to the children.

They pulled away from her, then stood, looking guilty and remorseful. They'd expected a scolding. They deserved one, too. All the way over here, he'd been practicing the tongue-lashing he was going to give them.

But instead he said, "It's a good thing Shayla called me before I found you were gone. I would have had a heart attack."

"Are you mad at us?" Cathy asked in a tiny voice.

"A little." He glanced toward Shayla, adding, "But the main thing is you're both all right."

Shayla gave the girls a tiny push from behind, and they started across the room.

He looked at the children again. "When we get home, we're going to have a long talk about rules and the consequences of breaking them. Deal?"

They nodded.

He gave them each a tight hug.

As he released them, Angie tugged on his shirtsleeve, then crooked her finger at him. He leaned down, and she whispered in his ear, "We were just tryin' to help."

"Help what?" he whispered back.

"With you marryin' her. You said you needed help."

For a moment, he didn't understand. Once he did, he couldn't help smiling. Well, the little imps. Six years old and already playing the matchmaker. Now how did a fella stay angry when their motive was such a good one?

He straightened, wiping the grin off his face as he did

so. "You two go get in the truck. Don't dawdle. Hear me?"

"Yes, Uncle Ian."

He waited until they were off the deck before he said, "I'm sorry they bothered you."

"They weren't a bother."

He raised an eyebrow to indicate his skepticism.

"Don't be too hard on them. They didn't mean any harm. It's just—" She stopped abruptly, as if suddenly realizing she was advising him on how to treat his nieces.

"I appreciate your advice, Shayla. You know that."

She shook her head. "It isn't my place."

It could be, he thought, but he managed not to say it. He'd rushed in too quickly before. He wasn't going to do it again.

"Tell the girls I'll see them at the fireworks tonight," she said.

It was obvious those kids were her weak spot. He was convinced of it. It might not be fair, but he intended to use this newfound knowledge for all it was worth. Cathy and Angie seemed willing enough to play their parts.

"You are taking them, aren't you?" she added. "To the fireworks?"

He frowned, as if seriously considering not attending the town's annual Fourth of July celebration. "I probably shouldn't allow them to go. After all, they ought to be punished for running off the way they did."

"Oh, no. It's the Fourth. You mustn't keep them home."

"Too harsh?"

"Well, maybe just a little bit. They miss their parents, and they're just starting to settle in to their unfamiliar surroundings. They should have this chance to meet other children. Perhaps you could make them…'' Again she let her words drift into silence. A blush brightened her cheeks.

"Go ahead. Tell me your suggestions."

"You need to do whatever you think's right. You're their uncle." She glanced over her shoulder at her computer, then back at him.

It was an obvious dismissal, and he decided not to press his luck. "Thanks again for calling me. See you tonight." He turned and left.

Picnic tables at the town park were covered with a vast array of foods—ham and fried chicken, baked beans and potato salad, Jell-O and sliced fruits, chips and dips, pies and cakes and cookies galore, and much, much more.

Families and friends gathered in the shade of old, misshapen trees, seated on folding chairs and blankets. The air was resplendent with conversations and laughter as longtime residents shared stories with relative newcomers, stories—nearly as old as the valley itself—that had been repeated time and time again through the years.

Cathy and Angie had no trouble making friends. It didn't hurt that they were the only twins in Rainbow Valley. Add to that Angie's bandaged head and the "war stories" of how it had happened, and they quickly became the center of attention of the younger set.

With his plate piled high with food, Ian watched the twins interacting with the other children. If he hadn't seen the transformation himself, he wouldn't have believed these were the same two girls who had returned with him to the ranch after their parents' departure. Those kids had done nothing but cry and wail and make mischief. These two were all smiles. Not that he didn't think there would be more homesick scenes ahead, but the worst seemed to be behind them.

And he had Shayla to thank for that.

With his gaze, he sought her out, finding her on a blanket with Ty and Anne on the opposite side of the park. She was watching the children as he had been just a moment before.

"What is it you're so afraid of?" he whispered.

As if she'd heard him, she looked in his direction. Their gazes met for a fraction of a second, and then she glanced away. But the brief exchange was enough to keep hope alive in his heart, for he was certain he saw his own feelings mirrored in her eyes. She cared for him much more than she was willing to admit.

I'm not giving up, Shayla, he told her silently.

He considered his options as he ate his supper, trying to figure the best way to overcome her objections. Unfortunately he was no expert at figuring out women. He'd failed miserably in his marriage, and his track record with the women he'd dated since Joanne's death seemed to say he hadn't learned much in the ensuing years.

But he didn't care about whether or not he'd figured out those other women. He only cared about understanding Shayla. Her resistance to him was more than just her not being ready for marriage. It was even more than her wanting to realize a dream, although that was part of it. But it went deeper than that, and he longed to know and understand. He wanted to be a part of her life, her whole life.

How did he convince her of that? How did he make her see that together they would both be better individuals than they were separately?

His gaze slid to Anne. He hadn't cared much for her

when she'd first arrived because he'd thought her vain and spoiled. He suspected he hadn't been completely wrong in that assessment. But Anne also loved and admired her older sister and was fiercely protective of her. She would want whatever would make Shayla happy.

Anne Vincent would be a good person to have in his corner, and he thought she might already be there.

He grinned. That made it five—himself, the twins, Anne, and Ty—against one.

How could Shayla resist them all?

"Don't you think Ian must be lonely over there?" Anne asked.

Despite herself, Shayla glanced in his direction. He looked very different in his T-shirt, Bermuda shorts and sandals. Very unlike the cowboy she was used to seeing, but still incredibly handsome.

"Maybe we should invite him to join us," her sister added.

She returned her gaze to Anne. "He isn't lonely. He knows everybody in the valley."

"Hmm." Anne rose from the blanket.

"Where are you going?"

"For more dessert." Anne smiled. "Want some?"

She shook her head, feeling foolish.

"How about you, Ty?" her sister continued.

"No thanks." He patted his stomach as he leaned back on his arms, his legs stretched out before him. "I'm too full to eat another bite."

Anne strolled toward the food tables, and more than a few heads turned as she walked by.

"Your sister must have a hollow leg," Ty commented. "Never seen a gal put away as much grub as she can and still stay so skinny."

''That's what our mother always said.''

Ty removed his hat and set it on the blanket beside him, then lay flat on his back and stared up at the cloudless blue sky, his hands now cradling his head. ''So how's that book comin'?''

''Okay.''

''Been kinda hard with Anne here, I take it.''

She shrugged. ''A little.''

''Plenty of excitement over at Paradise, now that the twins have come for a spell.''

She glanced across the park, but Ian was no longer where he'd been. Disappointment stung her heart.

''Don't know how Ian's coping so good. Last thing I'd want, if I was in his place, would be to get saddled with a couple of youngsters for a year. He's got plenty to do as it is, running the ranch. Now he says he's gotta find somebody to watch 'em during the day while he's working. What's he know about hiring a baby-sitter? Will you tell me that?''

She wished Ty would change the subject. She didn't want to talk about Ian. She didn't want to think about him, either. But she continued to scan the park for some sign of him.

She looked in vain. She couldn't find him anywhere.

Ian leaned against a large tree, which was gnarled and twisted with age, glad for the shade and surprised no one else had claimed this spot before him. The melody of Rainbow Brook, shallow and lined with smooth stones, sang softly as it cut through the northwest corner of the town park.

From this vantage point, he could observe Cathy and Angie on the playground equipment while maintaining an unobstructed view of Shayla and Ty, as well.

"She can be stubborn at times," Anne said as she appeared beside him.

He wasn't surprised to see her.

She smiled a bit ruefully. "We're a thoughtless lot."

"Who?"

"My brothers and sisters and me. Even our folks sometimes. We've gotten used to Shayla taking care of us, so we just assume she wants to and always will. She's good at it, too. Taking care of the needs of others."

"She's good at a lot of things."

"She *is* in love with you, you know."

His gaze returned to Shayla. "Then why does she resist me so hard?"

"Maybe I'd better tell you some family history. She probably hasn't bothered to."

"Only a little," he answered. "Not as much as I'd like to know."

"Then let me fill in the spaces. Our parents didn't have anything when they got married, and never had much since, either. Shayla was a honeymoon baby. Arrived nine months to the day after the wedding ceremony. Dad loves to tell everybody that. Mom lost a couple of babies after Shayla, and they were beginning to think they might not ever have any more children. Then when Shayla was eight, my brother Dwight was born. The rest of us followed at pretty regular intervals after that."

He nodded. "Seven of you in all."

"Shayla was always the baby-sitter and the diaper changer. Money was scarce and Mom had to have help with the kids and the laundry and the housework. So it fell to Shayla because she was so much older than the rest of us. And we just kept on expecting her to look after us, even once she was an adult." Anne moved to the opposite side of the tree as she spoke, then assumed a similar position to his, leaning against the trunk while staring across the park toward her sister. "She never could get away from us. Not even after she moved out of the house into a place of her own. We were always crashing at her apartment for one reason or another, and she let us because she loves us."

He nodded again. None of this was a surprise to him.

"Did you know she thinks she's unattractive?"

"But that isn't true."

"Well, *I* know it isn't true, but all that matters is, *she* thinks it is. And the sort of guys she's dated haven't helped matters. The last jerk just wanted a mommy for his kids, not a woman he could love."

"She deserves better."

"Yes."

They remained silent for several minutes, each lost in private thoughts.

Anne was the first to speak again. "Have you ever read any of her stuff?"

"No."

"Neither had I till I came here. Heck, most of us never even had a clue that she *wanted* to write a book, and when she told us, we brushed it off as unimportant." She lowered her voice. "I'm ashamed of us all."

Ian glanced at Anne. There were tears clinging to her lower lashes.

"She's good, Ian. When she was over cleaning your house the other day, I read her manuscript. I'm no expert, but I do read all the time, and I think she's got real talent. She could sell this thing. She could really go places."

To be brutally honest, that's what Ian was afraid of. That Shayla could really go places....

Like right out of this valley and out of his life.

Shayla helped clear the tables of leftovers, putting food away in coolers and picnic baskets. By the time she returned to the blanket, Anne was back and deep in conversation with Ty. Cathy and Angie were there, as well.

"Where's your uncle?" The question slipped out before Shayla could stop herself from asking it.

"Over at the truck, I think," Cathy answered, waving her hand toward the parking area. "He said we needed to find a spot to watch the fireworks from, and we told him we wanted to sit with you."

"You did?"

"Yeah, and he said that was okay with him."

She didn't know whether to be dismayed or relieved by the news. She'd spent the better part of the afternoon wishing she was with Ian, feeling alone and lonely. But how would she feel once he was nearby?

"Shayla?" Angie took hold of her hand.

Distracted, her eyes searching the parking lot for some sign of Ian, she replied, "Hmm?"

"You'll let us come to see you sometimes, won't you? Uncle Ian says we can't ever come over to your place again without asking first."

That got her attention. She knelt on the blanket. "Of course you can come over. But your uncle is right. You must call first, and an adult must bring you."

"Uncle Ian'll bring us any time we ask," Cathy piped in. "I know he will because he wants to see you, too."

Shayla felt equal parts pleasure and despair. It would be better if she didn't see him, but she longed to all the same.

"We can't go visit until we're through being grounded." Angie nudged her twin. "Remember?"

"Grounded, huh?"

"Yes." With wide eyes and pure drama in her voice, Cathy said, "And if he ever catches us near that old bull or the highway, he says he'll skin us alive and tan our hides on the side of the barn."

Shayla couldn't help it. She laughed aloud. "Is that what he told you?"

"That's *exactly* what I told them."

Her heart caught as she glanced over her shoulder to see Ian standing behind her.

"And as you can see," he continued, "it scared 'em plumb to death. For about fifteen seconds."

The twins giggled, revealing just how frightened of their uncle they were. Apparently, conditions between the three of them had dramatically improved.

Ian rounded the blanket, then sat down beside Angie. "How's your head?" he asked her.

"Fine."

"Doesn't hurt?" He touched the edge of the bandage.

"Nope."

He looked up, meeting Shayla's gaze. "She's played pretty hard this afternoon. Guess it didn't hurt her."

"Kids are resilient."

"I'm glad you decided to come." He gave her one of those slow smiles that could melt her heart.

Pleasure rushed through her, pooling in the pit of her stomach. "So am I."

For several heartbeats, they continued to stare into one another's eyes. Then Ian looked away, returning his attention to the twins.

"Either of you think you'll need your sweaters after

it gets dark?'' he asked. ''If so, we'd better get them before the fireworks begin.''

''We'll be fine.''

''No way. It's not cold.''

He'll make a wonderful father someday, Shayla thought, then silently added, *when he finds the right woman.*

He'd said *she* was the woman he wanted. Was that true? Or did he think so only because she was nearby, because she was the ''expert'' on children, because he hadn't met someone more suited to him?

Yet, if he really *did* love her...

She suddenly wished she'd stayed at the cabin. Things were clearer to her there; she knew precisely what she wanted and where she was going.

But whenever she was near Ian, all was confusion.

Ian didn't watch the fireworks that night. His gaze remained locked on Shayla.

She lay on her back, her arms serving as a pillow beneath her head. The twins lay on either side of her, mirroring her position. With each successive explosion of light and color, they oohed and aahed, as expected. Shayla could see all sorts of images in the glittering night sky, and she soon had the two girls playing with her.

''Look, there's an elephant!''

''There's a snake!''

''I see a mountain. See? Do you see it, too?''

But no matter what imaginary animal or scene the three of them discovered, no matter how many times they encouraged him to look up, Ian had eyes only for Shayla.

She appeared especially lovely tonight. It amazed him

that she thought herself unattractive. What could have caused her to see herself that way? Even when he'd suspected her of being not all right in the head, that first day he'd seen her, he'd still thought she was cute. *Odd, but cute.* He remembered thinking those very words.

But *cute* wasn't a good enough word to describe the Shayla he'd come to know in recent weeks. She was special, unique, pretty to behold and beautiful in heart and spirit.

He watched her turn to the right and whisper something in Angie's ear. The little girl laughed, then nodded.

"What?" Cathy asked as she sat up, not wanting to be left out.

Shayla crooked an index finger, indicating for Cathy to lean down. Then she whispered in her ear. Cathy grinned and nodded before lying back down.

Ian wondered what the secret was, but he wasn't going to ask.

Shayla was a natural with kids. It was easy to see why her siblings took her for granted. She was a bit of a surrogate mother to them, and all kids take advantage of their parents in one way or another, in his opinion.

A succession of bright fireworks lit up the sky. Shayla clapped her hands.

That was just one of the things that made him love her—the way she took pleasure in simple things. It's why he could hope she would be content in Rainbow Valley. It was why he was willing to take the chance of again asking her to marry him.

Resist me all you want, Shayla Vincent. I'm not ready to give up yet.

Chapter Fourteen

Shayla cracked one eye open, saw the light of day streaming through the bedroom curtains and muttered, "Did anyone get the license number of that semi?" Then she rolled onto her other side and covered her head with the blanket.

What a horrible night!

She'd been tortured by dreams. Strange, disjointed dreams of flying horses and charging bulls, puppies and calves and colts, crying children and tall dark-haired cowboys bathed in the light of fireworks. She remembered running, as if being chased, but never knowing who or what pursued her.

Strangest of all, she had dreamed she was in the huge kitchen at Paradise, preparing Thanksgiving dinner— roast turkey, baked yams, peas with pearl onions, hand-mashed potatoes with gravy, and several kinds of pie. She'd looked like a 1950s housewife, complete with a shirtwaist dress and petticoats and a string of faux pearls around her neck. Whatever had she eaten to cause such silliness?

Then she remembered dreaming that her computer had been missing, her entire manuscript lost. She groaned as she tossed off the blanket. She wouldn't know a moment's peace until she went out to the living room and made certain everything was where it was supposed to be.

Muttering to herself about insanity and the signs thereof, she yanked on her bathrobe, slid her feet into her house slippers and opened her bedroom door. The wonderful aroma of coffee met her instantly. Anne was already up. Was it *that* late in the morning?

"Hey, sleepyhead," her sister greeted as Shayla shuffled down the hall.

Before she answered, she glanced toward her desk, verifying her computer had not been stolen while she slept. That confirmed, she mumbled, "Morning," and made a beeline for the kitchen and a cup of java.

"I was beginning to wonder if you were ever getting up."

"What time is it?" She filled a large mug with coffee.

"Almost nine."

"*Nine?*" Shayla turned toward the clock on the wall.

Anne laughed. "That's what I thought. You *never* sleep in this late."

"I had a rough night."

Thankfully Anne didn't inquire what had made it so. Instead she said, "Well, Ty is driving me down to Boise. He's got the day off. We plan to do some shopping at the mall and who knows what else. Maybe see a show at the big movie complex they've got there. Twenty-one theaters. Lots of choices. Want to come along?"

"No, thanks."

"Didn't think you would. Just as well anyway. I've got a bad crush on this cowboy, and I don't need a big sister acting as chaperone when I want to be alone with him. If you know what I mean, and I think you do."

Shayla looked at Anne over the top of her mug as she took a sip of coffee. Yes, she knew what her sister meant.

Anne laughed again. "Don't worry. I'll be on my best behavior."

"Sure you will." As she turned away, she whispered, "Everybody's on their best behavior when they're twenty-one."

"I heard that," her sister called in a singsong voice as she ran up the stairs.

A short while later, Ty came for Anne, then the cabin was silent once again. Shayla settled in at the computer, clad in one of her baggy T-shirts and a loose-fitting pair of shorts, her coffee mug close at hand. She worked furiously, trying to immerse herself in her story, determined to think of nothing else.

Especially not of Ian.

Except she did think of him. Because the hero of her novel, Chet Morrison, was a dead ringer for Ian O'Connell. So every time she typed Chet's name, it was Ian whom she pictured in her mind. And the beautiful, buxom, sexy True was the person Shayla *wanted* to be.

All of a sudden, she wondered who was going to cook Thanksgiving dinner for Ian, Cathy and Angie, come the fourth Thursday in November.

"Oh, brother," she muttered. "This has got to stop."

She tried to concentrate on her book again…and failed.

Ty had the day off. So what were Ian and the twins

doing? Maybe they'd gone to the lake again. Maybe they'd gone for a horseback ride.

"What happened to *my* riding lessons?"

Her eyes widened. She couldn't believe she'd just said that.

"This is getting ridiculous. I have completely lost my mind. It's impractical and destined for disaster."

She pressed Save, then closed out of her program, quite certain she was done writing for the day.

Calling herself every name for a fool that she could think of, she grabbed her purse, went out to the car and drove to Paradise Ranch.

If he was lucky, he would die before noon.

Ian lay on the cool tile of the bathroom floor, too weak to crawl to his bed, too sick to go far from the toilet. He didn't know if it was something he'd eaten or the stomach flu. Whatever it was, he hoped it was over soon. Death didn't seem a bad option at the moment.

Through the heating vent, he heard Cathy and Angie talking to each other. He wondered where they were, what they were doing, if they were okay.

He should call someone. The girls were too young to be alone. And if he *did* die—which felt like a real possibility—someone would have to look after them until their parents could get back to the States.

He didn't know how long it was before he heard the uncertain voice from nearby.

"Uncle Ian?"

He started to open his eyes, then thought better of it the minute the room began to spin.

"Would you like some chicken soup? That's what Mommy gives us when we're sick."

He moaned in answer. The very idea of food made him want to upchuck again.

They must have understood, for they left.

He should have told them to call Shayla. Why hadn't he thought of it before it was too late? Who knew what they might do while he was lying there, unable to move? What if they toppled something else over on top of them? What if this time the injury was more serious than what had happened last week?

The phone. He needed to reach the bedside phone.

Squeezing his eyes tight against the weaving and swirling, he struggled to rise. He managed to get to his feet while gripping the open shower door.

Now, just put one foot in front of another, he told himself. Just one after another.

He made it a distance of about four feet. Then the floor seemed to disappear from beneath him. He felt himself tumbling, falling, pitching toward some dark, bottomless pit.

"Ian!"

He thought that sounded like Shayla, but it was too late to find out as he sank into that black pit.

Shayla tried to reach Ian in time to break his fall. She wasn't fast enough. He hit the floor with a frightening thud.

She turned toward the twins, feigning a calm she didn't feel. "Girls, I need a large glass of ice water. Do you think you can get it for me? There's ice and water in the refrigerator door, and those large plastic glasses in the cupboard next to the sink. Like the ones you had for the picnic yesterday? Can you do that for me?"

"Sure. We can get it."

"Is Uncle Ian gonna be okay?"

"Yes. Now go on, and be very careful getting that glass out of the cupboard. One of you hold the step stool while the other climbs up to get the glass."

"Okay."

She waited until they were out of sight, then dashed to Ian's side. He was pale as a sheet. Her palm on his forehead confirmed her suspicions. He was burning up with a fever.

"Ian? It's Shayla. Ian, can you hear me?"

His eyelids fluttered, but he didn't open them.

"Ian, try to look at me. Wake up and look at me."

He seemed to be coming around.

She stood and went into the bathroom. She held a washcloth under cold running water, then wrung it out before returning to kneel next to him.

"Ian, look at me." She laid the folded cloth on his forehead. "Come on. Wake up."

Finally he opened his eyes. They appeared glazed, glassy, unfocused.

"Can you see me?"

"Sort of." His voice was hoarse and nearly inaudible.

"The twins said you've been in here forever."

He groaned. "Not all that long…I don't think. Just since…early this morning."

"Can we get you onto the bed?"

"I don't know." He moistened his fever-chapped lips with the tip of his tongue. "Let's find out."

She scooted across the floor to position herself at his head. Then she placed her knees up against his shoulders and leaned forward, sliding her hands beneath him. "I'll lift you slowly. Don't try to hurry. Just get your bearings. Okay?"

"Okay."

They seemed to be doing fine. At least until it was

time to help him stand. Then Shayla wondered if her plan was such a good one. He was heavier than he looked. But somehow they managed to keep him upright long enough to reach the bed, a thankfully short distance from where he'd fallen.

The girls returned a moment after Ian's head hit the pillow, his eyes already closed again, a clammy sweat beading his forehead.

"Here's the water," Cathy said, holding out the glass to Shayla. "We put in lots of ice."

"Thanks." She took it from the girl, then leaned down toward Ian. "Cathy and Angie brought you some cold water. Can you take a sip?"

"I think I'd rather just…lie here…for a while," he whispered. "Nice and still."

"Okay. I'll be back in a little bit to check on you." She straightened. "Come on, girls. Let's let your uncle get some rest, shall we?"

"Are you sure he's gonna be okay?" Angie asked as they left the bedroom and descended the stairs.

"I'm sure." She wasn't sure at all. She planned to call the doctor as soon as she had the children fed.

From the condition of the kitchen, it was obvious the twins had fixed their own breakfast that morning. Dry cereal was scattered on the floor, and the milk carton still sat on the counter next to the refrigerator, tiny white puddles pooling nearby.

"Help me tidy up," she told them, "and then I'll make some grilled cheese sandwiches for lunch."

"Good. I'm hungry."

"Me, too."

"Me, three," Shayla said, forcing a smile she didn't feel. "Cathy, you get a dishcloth and wipe off the table.

Angie, you grab the broom and sweep up the cereal. I'll clean the counter and stovetop.''

It didn't take them long to put things right. The twins were more help than she'd expected them to be. Within fifteen minutes, Shayla had the girls seated at the kitchen table, eating their sandwiches. Then she slipped away to use the phone in Ian's office. The doctor's receptionist put her right through to Dr. Dobbins, and Shayla quickly explained to him what she had found when she'd arrived at Paradise.

''I'll be out that way later this afternoon,'' Dr. Dobbins told her. ''But I wouldn't worry if I were you. Just try to give him aspirin for the fever and plenty of fluids so he doesn't get dehydrated.''

''I will.''

''I should be there about two. Three o'clock at the latest.''

''Thank you, Dr. Dobbins. I appreciate it.''

''No problem. And don't worry, Miss Vincent.''

After placing the receiver in its cradle, Shayla returned to the kitchen. The twins were polishing off the last of their grilled cheese sandwiches. She joined them at the table and took a bite of her own sandwich, now cold and a bit soggy, but she scarcely noticed. She was too deep in thought.

She didn't know much about ranching, but she knew there were chores to be done every single day, come rain or come shine. Anne had told her both Ty and Mick, the other ranch hand, were given the day off. That meant Ian had intended to handle all the necessary chores by himself. And since he was sick, that meant they hadn't been done.

''I guess the first thing we'd better do,'' she said aloud, ''is check on the animals.''

The twins looked at her expectantly.

"Have you helped your uncle with any of the chores since you got here?"

They shook their heads.

Darn. She'd hoped for a different answer.

"Well, we'd better see what we can do." She took one more bite, then rose from her chair. "Come on."

"But you didn't finish eating," Cathy pointed out.

"I guess I wasn't hungry."

"Maybe Uncle Ian would like it," Angie suggested.

"I doubt it."

Shayla led the way out of the house. The first thing she heard was the barking of dogs. When the kennels came into view, they really went wild, whining and jumping in excitement.

"You poor things," Shayla crooned. "Closed up for so long. Good Coira. Good Bonny. Good Belle." As she spoke, she opened the gates to each pen and let them out.

Cathy and Angie joined Shayla in petting the dogs and reassuring them.

"Let's find the dog food, shall we? They must be starved by now." She patted Belle's head again. "Good thing your puppies are all in new homes. Huh, girl?"

After finding where the dog food was stored, Shayla filled the dogs' water and food dishes, and went into the barn. She hadn't been worried about messing up too badly when it came to feeding the dogs, but the livestock were another matter. She was relieved to find only one stall occupied. Better yet, the horse in it was the ever-gentle Pumpkin.

Water, she told herself. Water was always the first priority.

She found a pump with a hose attached outside the

south door of the barn. The other end of the hose had a spray nozzle so she assumed it was safe to raise the lever on the pump. Thankfully she was correct.

So far, so good.

Speaking softly to Pumpkin, she opened the gate and went in. It took only a moment to refill the reservoir in the corner. The mare nickered, as if in appreciation.

"You're probably hungry, too. Aren't you, Pumpkin?"

Another nicker, accompanied by a bob of the head.

By this time, Cathy and Angie had climbed up on the side of the stall and were observing from above the top rail.

"Do you have any idea how much hay a horse needs?" she asked them while stroking the mare's muzzle.

"Nope."

"Neither do I," she confessed. "I suppose I'd better ask your uncle. I don't need a sick horse on my hands, too."

She exited the stall, then went to shut off the water pump. When she returned, she called for the twins to join her outside the barn.

Once there, she placed a hand on each of their shoulders. "You two stay put. Right here. Throw a stick for the dogs or something. I'm going inside to ask your uncle a few questions. I want to find you here when I get back. Understood?"

They answered in the affirmative.

"Good. I'll be back in a jiff."

Ian wished somebody would stop the world so he could get off. Or, at the very least, if they could just stop the room from spinning like a top.

"Ian?"

Reluctantly he opened his eyes. He hadn't dreamed Shayla's voice. She was standing beside his bed. Prettiest thing he'd seen in a month of Sundays.

She offered a tentative smile. "How are you feeling? Any better?"

She placed her hand on his forehead; it felt cool against his feverish skin. He wished she'd leave it there. Her touch was comforting.

"Any better?" she asked again.

"You don't want to know."

Her smile grew a fraction.

"The girls?"

"They're fine. We're seeing to the animals now. I fed the dogs and let them out for a run. And I put water in Pumpkin's stall." A tiny frown furrowed her forehead. "But I don't know how much hay to feed her."

"A couple of flakes." He had to close his eyes again. The spinning was getting worse, and the last thing he wanted was to empty his stomach in front of Shayla.

"Flakes?" She touched his shoulder. "How much is that, Ian? What's a flake of hay?"

Somehow he managed to lift his arms, placing his hands an appropriate distance apart. At least, he hoped it was an accurate measurement. With his eyes closed and everything tilting and whirling, it was hard to tell.

"About this much off the bale," he whispered.

She must have understood him. She must also have sensed his need to be quiet, for she slipped away without another word.

He would have to properly thank her later. Much later.

Chapter Fifteen

Ian was going to live after all.

When he awakened early the next morning, he discovered his bedroom had ceased to behave like a carousel and was once again stationary. A good sign. But his mouth tasted like a herd of cattle had been driven through it. He needed a toothbrush and toothpaste. Bad!

He shoved aside the sheet, slid his legs over the edge of the mattress and sat up slowly. So far, so good. He let his feet touch the floor, then took a deep breath before standing. The room lurched a bit, then righted itself. He took another deep breath.

He was rarely sick—maybe a cold every year or two, if that—and he resented the weakness he felt after this bout with the flu. He especially hated the idea that Shayla had seen him like this. Not exactly the best way to impress a woman, in his book. But he would be eternally grateful for the help she'd rendered yesterday.

At least, he thought she'd rendered it. Things were a bit fuzzy in his head yet. Maybe he'd only imagined her cool hand on his hot forehead. Maybe he'd only dreamed her gentle smile as she'd leaned over him. Maybe he just thought she'd pitched in to help in whatever way she could.

On slightly shaky legs, he made his way to the bathroom. One glance in the mirror, and he was sorry he'd looked. "Death warmed over" would be an apt description.

He leaned his thighs against the bathroom counter for support, then proceeded to brush his teeth, mentally thanking the guy who'd invented mint-flavored toothpaste. Next, he shaved the two-day-old stubble off his face, and afterward he combed his hair.

The results weren't great, but he was at least presentable.

He remembered the doctor helping him out of the clothes he'd put on yesterday morning and into the pajama bottoms he wore now. He considered getting dressed, then rejected the idea. Ty and Mick would arrive in another hour or two. They could handle whatever chores needed doing.

With his strength rapidly draining, he finished up in the bathroom and returned to his bed, dropping onto it with a sigh of relief. He felt as if he'd put in a full day on the range.

A soft rap sounded at his door. He turned his head on the pillow and looked in that direction just as Shayla entered, carrying a tray.

"I heard you get up," she told him, "and I thought you might want some toast and juice."

"You stayed the night?" But it didn't really surprise

him. As sick as he'd been, she wouldn't have left the twins alone.

She set the tray on his nightstand, then leaned over to feel his forehead. "A bit clammy. No fever. That's a good sign." She smiled.

That smile. It was worth being sick just to see it. Man, how he loved her.

"Do you think you can eat something?"

He'd do anything she asked. "I'll give it a try."

"Let me help you sit up."

He'd made it to the bathroom and back by himself. He was pretty certain he could have sat up by himself, too. But he didn't try. Not when Shayla was such a good nurse, fluffing the pillow to put behind his back, making sure the tray was just so on his lap, asking him if there was anything else he needed.

"No," he answered. "Just stay and tell me what all happened yesterday. Did the girls think to call you? Is that why you showed up here?"

She sat on the side of the mattress, not too close to him. "No." She glanced toward the window. "I just happened to come over." She paused again, then met his gaze. "They were two very frightened little girls. They thought you were dying."

"So did I for a while."

"Dr. Dobbins said you had a temp of a hundred and three."

"You were in here most of the night. Weren't you? Bathing my forehead, giving me sips of water."

Her smile was shy, and a blush tinted her cheeks.

"I thought I was dreaming."

She looked away a second time. "You needed help." She shrugged. "And the girls couldn't be left alone."

He reached over and took hold of her hand. "You're always helping somebody, aren't you, Shayla?"

Her blush brightened; she avoided his eyes.

"Me. Cathy and Angie. Anne. Always somebody else." He lowered his voice. "No wonder you feel like it's time to take care of yourself for a change." He tightened his fingers. "I'd like to help take care of you, too. If you'd just give me a chance."

She rose abruptly. "I think I heard the girls. They'll need their breakfast. I'll be back for the tray. Eat something."

He'd struck a nerve, he realized as he watched her leave the room.

And maybe he'd knocked a small hole in the wall of her resistance.

At the top of the stairs, Shayla stopped and leaned her back against the wall. Her heart was racing, and her stomach was all aflutter.

Maybe she was getting the flu now, she thought as she pressed the palms of her hands against her abdomen.

But she knew she wasn't sick. She was in love. Horribly, wonderfully, completely and helplessly in love.

The question was, what was she going to do about it?

And that same question kept repeating itself in her head throughout the morning as she fed the children, did several loads of laundry, cleaned the kitchen and dusted and vacuumed the entire downstairs. Even after Anne came to watch the children while Shayla went home to shower and change, she couldn't stop thinking it.

What *was* she going to do about loving Ian?

He wanted to marry her. He said he wanted to take care of her. He loved her.

She'd thought at first he was still in love with the

memory of Joanne, but she believed now she'd been wrong about that. He seemed earnest when he said he loved her. And when he looked at her with those brown eyes of his, something inside her melted, and she was left defenseless. He had no idea what he did to her.

Or did he?

So if she was sure he loved her, and she knew she loved him, what was the problem? Why didn't she simply say yes and let him take care of her?

Staying in his home last night, sitting beside his bed, watching him sleep, it had been easy to imagine herself as his wife. She had toyed with the fantasy throughout much of the night, envisioning herself in that very same bed, picturing his arms around her as he drew her close against him, her head on his shoulder, both of them replete after passionate lovemaking.

Why not? Why couldn't she have that? Didn't she *want* to be a wife? *Ian's* wife?

For two days she wrestled with her thoughts and emotions. For two days she struggled to discover what was the right thing to do, for herself and for Ian. For two days she divided her time between the ranch and the cabin. She took care of the twins. She cooked for Ian, who was no longer too weak to get out of bed. She even managed to write another chapter on her book. She did any number of chores.

But most of all she sought answers from her heart.

Early on Friday evening, she returned to Paradise, no more settled in her mind and heart than she'd been three days before.

"You didn't have to come back," Anne told her. "I would have been glad to stay overnight with the children so you could write."

Shayla shook her head. "I couldn't seem to concentrate. I might as well be here."

"She wants to be with Uncle Ian," Cathy said with a note of authority.

Anne grinned. "I think you're right, half-pint."

"I have *work* to do," Shayla pointed out. "I *am* the housekeeper."

Her sister rolled her eyes.

"Go home, Anne."

Anne leaned toward the twins and, in a stage whisper, said, "She's in a foul mood, isn't she?"

The girls nodded, both of them grinning.

"Oh, brother," Shayla muttered as she turned and headed for the closet in the front hall.

She retrieved the vacuum, then carried it up the stairs into the studio. The bookcase that Cathy had knocked over the night Angie was hurt had been righted the next day and all the books long since put back in place. And since the room was never used, there was little cleaning to be done.

Leaving the vacuum near the door, she walked over to the paintings of Ian. He'd been much younger when Joanne painted him, but his wife had foreseen the man he would become.

There was strength and determination in his unlined, youthful face. There was integrity in his eyes. This was a man who knew how to take life as it came. This was a man as strong and unshakable as the mountains that cradled this valley. This was a man who took pleasure in the green of the grass, the blue of the sky, the song of a meadowlark, the nobility of an elk. A man who could hold a child in his arms and wipe away tears with gentle fingertips. A man who could kiss a woman until he'd stolen the very breath from her. This was a man with a heart as big as all outdoors, a man capable of so much love.

She reached out, briefly touching his image on one of the canvasses.

And suddenly it didn't seem so impossible.

Suddenly she felt a ray of hope.

Something was different about Shayla.

Ian sensed it the instant he saw her standing in the studio, staring at the portraits. It wasn't anything he could define exactly. It wasn't the way she looked or moved or anything she did. But something was different about her, all the same.

He cleared his throat. She turned toward him.

"I thought Anne was staying with the girls today," he said.

She shrugged.

"You staying the night again?"

She nodded.

"You don't need to, you know. I'm almost a hundred percent."

"I think you'll rest better if you don't have to concern yourself with the children."

He lifted an eyebrow but didn't argue with her reasoning.

"You are looking much better," she said.

"Like I said, I'm nearly one hundred percent."

She gave him a hesitant smile, then turned away and walked over to the window. "There's a nice breeze this evening. Is it all right if I open this?"

"Sure." He took a step into the studio. What was going on in that pretty head of hers? he wondered.

Shayla opened the window as wide as it would go.

She remained there, staring up at the mountainside as the day began to wane.

After a long while, she said, "It's beautiful here. The trees. The mountains. It always smells so good. I wonder how your mother and sister could leave it."

For a split second, Ian thought his fever had returned. Was he hallucinating or did she mean what he thought she meant?

"I don't reckon it was easy for either of them, but they had their reasons." He took another step into the room. "Dad's health wasn't good, so he and Mom moved to a warmer climate. As for Leigh, she met and fell in love with Jim. His work was elsewhere, and she chose to be with him."

"That's what I would do. Choose to be with the man I love."

"Shayla? What is it you're saying?"

"I want to be a writer, Ian. I want it with all my heart." She turned to face him. "I've got all these characters in my head, and all these stories demanding to be told. Sometimes I think I'll go crazy from the need to get it all out onto paper. And I've waited so long for the opportunity to try." She waved her hand in a gesture of frustration. "No one's ever believed I could do it except me."

"And me. I believe in you. I always have."

She continued as if he hadn't spoken. "Thanks to Aunt Lauretta, it's here now, my chance to prove myself, and I've been working hard to take advantage of it. I think I can do it, too. I think I can write good books. Maybe great books. And I love writing. I do. I love it so very much. More than I ever thought I would."

He watched her, unconsciously holding his breath, waiting for her to go on.

Tears began to trace her cheeks. "But I think I love you even more."

He had her in his arms in a heartbeat. He kissed her before she could take the words back. He kissed her with all the pent-up longing he'd been feeling since the night she'd refused his proposal of marriage. He kissed her until they were both desperate for air. And even when he stopped kissing her, he didn't let her go. He held her close, burying his face in her curly hair.

He kissed the tear tracks on her cheeks, then whispered, "Say it again."

"Say what?" She clung to him, her cheek pressed against his chest.

"Say you love me."

"I love you." A tremulous smile curved her mouth. "I love you."

For a long time, he simply stared down at her, feeling awash in more emotions than he could name. He didn't want to do or say anything to spoil what was happening between them, and yet there was much still to be said. He couldn't avoid it forever.

"I've already bungled this a few times, one way or another," he began. "I'm afraid I'll do it again."

She gave her head a tiny shake.

"Shayla Vincent, I'm asking you to be my wife. And I swear to you, on my heart and my life and everything I hold dear, I'll always support you in the things you want to do. As long as you want to write your books, I'll do whatever you need to make it easier for you to do just that."

"Ian, I—"

"No, let me finish while I can." He drew a deep breath. "I'm not saying I'll be a perfect husband. Heaven knows, I'm bound to screw up plenty. I've already proven that. But my mistakes won't be made because I don't love you.''

''I know.''

He covered her lips with his index finger to keep her silent. ''I'll do my level best to always make you happy.'' He brought his face closer to hers, drowning himself in the deep blue of her eyes. ''So will you marry me, Shayla?''

''Yes.''

He blinked, afraid to believe that he'd heard her right. Afraid he might be dreaming the whole thing.

''Yes, Ian O'Connell, I'll marry you.''

Once again, he pulled her close for a long, deep kiss. He thought, Lord, if I'm dreaming, don't let me ever wake up.

It was the sound of whooping and hollering that broke them apart. They turned toward the window. Ian was certain the commotion could only mean trouble of some sort. Instead, what he found was Ty, Anne and the twins standing below the window, watching him and Shayla.

Ty tossed his hat into the air and let loose with an ear-splitting ''Yee-ha!''

Grinning from ear to ear, Anne applauded as she shouted, ''About time, you two.''

Cathy and Angie broke into giggles.

''She said yes!'' Ian yelled down at them.

''We heard,'' Ty answered.

''Wait there!'' Anne called. ''I've got to give you both a hug of congrats.'' She disappeared, followed by the twins and Ty.

Ian turned Shayla toward him.

''Looks like it'll be a while before we have another moment alone to do this,'' he said.

He kissed her, savoring the sweetness of her mouth and the warmth of her body, silently thanking heaven above for bringing her to Rainbow Valley just for him.

Chapter Sixteen

The old MacGregor house had been deserted almost fifteen years, the windows boarded over, Keep Out signs posted on the front and back doors. The interior was dark, dank and filled with cobwebs. They caught at Chet's hat, at his face, at his hands.

A floorboard creaked beneath his foot as he stepped into the parlor. He froze, listening. If the killer was still in the house, he now knew Chet was there, as well.

Nothing. No sound except for the wind whistling around the corner of the house.

He moved forward, his flashlight illuminating the way.

Deputy Caldwell had told Chet to stay out of this. Now that he was acting sheriff, in the wake of Sheriff Tuttle's murder, Caldwell was determined to proceed by the book.

But the deputy was too slow and methodical for Chet. He wasn't going to wait around until they found another *body. True's body. She meant too much to him. He wasn't going to leave any stone unturned until he found her, until he made certain she was safe.*

He opened a door and discovered the stairway to the cellar. Caldwell had said they'd searched the place from top to bottom. Maybe. But something in Chet's gut told him she was somewhere in this house.

"Hang on, True," he whispered under his breath. "Hang on a little bit longer."

He descended the steps into the dirt-floor cellar, pushing aside more cobwebs as he went. If Caldwell and the others had searched down here, he couldn't see any signs of it by his flashlight. It didn't look like anyone had been in this cellar in the past fifty years. Which would mean True wasn't down here, either.

He almost turned to leave, almost decided he was looking in the wrong place, almost gave up.

Then something caught his eye. He wasn't sure what. He wasn't sure why. But his pulse quickened and the hair on the back of his neck stood on end.

He trained his flashlight on the farthest corner. A section of the wall was a darker, richer brown than the rest.

His heart nearly stopped.

Freshly turned dirt.

He was down the remaining steps and across the cellar in no time.

"True!" He began digging and clawing at the wall with his bare hands. "True, hang on! I'm coming!"

Please, God, *he prayed silently.* Let me be in time.

"I know it's traditional to have the wedding in the bride's hometown," Shayla told her mother. "But Ian and I want to have the ceremony at the ranch."

"But, darling, all your friends are here in Portland."

There was no point in trying to explain to her mother that all of her real friends were right here in this valley.

"If you're worried about the cost of the airplane tickets for the whole family, Mom, I can chip in with the money Aunt Lauretta left me."

After a lengthy silence on the other end of the line, Reba said, "I certainly hope you know what you're doing. First this notion to be a mystery novelist instead of finding another job, and now you're rushing into marriage with a man you've known less than two months."

"This is not some sort of emotional crisis." Shayla tried to keep the frustration out of her voice. "I love Ian, and he loves me."

"Oh, honey, I'm sure you do. It's only...I don't want to see you get hurt."

Some of the tension drained from her. "I know that, Mom," she said softly. "But I'm thirty years old. I know what I'm doing. We aren't rushing into this blind. We just know it's right. My writing is going incredibly well, and Ian makes me happy. I've fallen in love with this valley and all the people in it."

"All right, Shayla. If this is what you want." A pause. "Here's your father."

"Hi, sweetheart."

"Hi, Dad."

"I take it we're coming to Idaho for the wedding?"

"Yes. Ian and I want an outdoor ceremony here at the ranch. I told Mom I could help pay for the tickets to fly all of you over."

"No need for that," her father said. "You hang on to your money. Lauretta didn't leave it to you so you could spend it on us. I can afford to do this. It isn't every day my firstborn gets married."

She swallowed the lump in her throat. "Thanks, Dad."

"Hey, sweetheart?"

"Yes?"

"We're happy for you. We're glad you've found the right guy. Anne says he's terrific."

"Yes, he is."

"You tell him I said he'd better be good to you."

"He is." She laughed softly. "But I'll still tell him."

"We'll call you in a few days. Just as soon as we know everybody's schedules."

"Okay."

"We love you, babe. Give Anne our love, too."

"I will. Bye, Dad. I love you."

Shayla hung up the telephone, feeling better after talking to her father. He might agree with her mother that Shayla was rushing into marriage, but at least he hadn't said so. And he was right about her having plenty to keep her busy. With less than a month until her wedding day, she knew it was only going to get busier.

Ian and the twins drove over to Shayla's cabin at noon. "So, what did your folks say?" he asked, immediately after kissing her.

"They were surprised, but happy for me. What about your mother?"

"Over the moon." He nibbled on her earlobe, ignoring Angie's and Cathy's snickers. "She can't wait to meet you."

"We talked to Mommy and Daddy last night," Cathy volunteered.

"We told Mommy we're gonna be your flower girls," Angie continued, "and she said we had to take lots and lots of pictures and send them to her."

Ian tightened his arms around Shayla. "I thought we'd better go talk to Pastor Barnett, make sure he's available to perform the ceremony on the eighth."

"We should have done that before calling our parents."

"Minor details." Unable to keep himself from it, he stole another kiss. If he had his druthers, he'd go right on kissing her till the cows came home.

She didn't seem inclined to stop him, either. In fact, she nestled in closer. A tiny moan of pleasure escaped her throat. The sound seemed to reverberate right through him, causing his heart to pound and his blood to boil.

Well, given the twins were present, he supposed it might be prudent to step back and cool off.

As he backed away, he saw that Shayla's face was flushed. She gazed at him with both desire and impatience, and he felt a ridiculous pride in knowing she wanted him as much as he wanted her. He wished they'd eloped instead of planning a more formal wedding. He was ready for her to move into his place now.

Today.

This minute.

Yesterday would have been even better.

She released a throaty laugh, as if she'd read his mind.

"When are we gonna get our dresses, Shayla?" one of the twins asked.

She turned toward the girls just in the nick of time. Otherwise, Ian would have pulled her back into his arms and started kissing her again.

Affectionately, Shayla brushed the hair away from Cathy's forehead. "Later this week we'll drive down to Boise, you and me and Anne."

"Can't I go, too?" Ian asked.

"No," the three females answered in unison, then giggled.

"Hmm. So that's how it's going to be." He tried to look suitably insulted.

Shayla slipped her arm around his waist. "Stop pouting, and let's go see Pastor Barnett."

"I'm not pouting."

"Ha!" Mischief twinkled in her eyes.

"You *were*, Uncle Ian. We saw you."

"I'm outnumbered," he grumbled, trying—and failing—to hide his grin.

He wondered if it was legal for a man to be this happy.

That evening, with the twins in bed and Ty and Anne off on a date somewhere, Ian and Shayla snuggled together on the front porch swing, his arm around her back, her head resting on his shoulder. A nearly full moon bathed the valley in a blanket of white light. Crickets serenaded from the pasture, accompanied by the *ribbitt, ribbitt* of frogs.

"Mmm," Shayla murmured. "What a perfect ending to a perfect day."

"My thoughts exactly."

"We may not have many evenings like this for a while. There's so much to be done to get ready for the wedding."

"We should have eloped."

She laughed softly. "That's about the tenth time you've said that today."

"Is it?" He kissed the top of her head. "Must be because I mean it." His breath was warm on her hair.

Tiny shivers ran up and down her spine, and gooseflesh formed on her arms.

"Mmm," she murmured again.

"I never expected this."

"What?"

"You. Being in love again. I hoped it would happen, but I just didn't believe it would. I didn't think I'd ever meet the right woman. I've been alone a long time."

She shifted in his arms, looking up at him. "Tell me about Joanne."

"What would you like to know?"

"Do you still love her?" The question slipped out before she could think better of it. And once it was spoken, the only thing she could do was hold her breath and wait for his answer.

Ian was silent for a long time, all the while staring down into her eyes.

At last he spoke, his voice low and filled with regret. "I loved Joanne. I'd be lying if I said I didn't. We were just kids when we got married, but we were happy for the most part. We were selfish in our own ways, too, like many young people who still think the universe revolves around them. We wanted different things, and neither of us knew how to compromise."

He looked in the direction of the highway, but judging by his expression, his mind was even farther away than that.

"I don't know what would have happened to our marriage if she'd lived," he continued. "I'm not sure we would have made it. Probably not." He paused. "No, I'm certain we would have been divorced before long."

"I'm sorry. I shouldn't have asked."

"Yes, you should have." His gaze returned to her. "I don't want there to be any secrets between us, Shayla. No unspoken questions. We should always talk about things openly."

She nodded, then returned her head to his shoulder.

They were silent for another long spell. A companionable silence, neither of them feeling compelled to speak, content to simply be together. He stroked her hair with the fingers of one hand. She circled her fingers on his chest, feeling the beat of his heart beneath her hand.

Finally he said, "You don't mind that it won't be just the two of us here after we're married, do you?"

"You mean, Cathy and Angie? No, I don't mind." She closed her eyes. "You're a wonderful uncle. At least, now that you're over that rocky start."

"I've always sort of hoped for kids of my own." There was an unspoken question in his words.

Shayla didn't know what to say. A few months ago— a few *weeks* ago—she'd thought she never wanted to have children. She'd figured she had already raised enough of them. But now? She wasn't sure. What would it be like to carry Ian's baby in her womb?

"I love you, Shayla," he whispered.

And what she thought he might be saying was, *It's okay. We don't have to decide about children now. We have time. We have the rest of our lives.*

At least that's what she hoped he meant.

A half an hour later, Ian watched the taillights of Shayla's car grow dimmer as she drove away from the house. When he knew she'd safely reached the highway, he turned and went inside. Once upstairs, he checked on the girls. They were sound asleep.

He stood at the side of the double bed, soft light from the hallway illuminating their faces. Angie's bandage was gone now, and it took him a moment to be sure who was who. He was kind of proud of himself that he was beginning to see the slight differences in their faces.

Shayla had noticed them right off, but it had taken him a bit longer.

He remembered that first twenty-four-hour period with these two little girls. He'd dubbed them the twin terrors. They'd scared him half to death with their tantrums and their tears. But they hadn't scared Shayla. She'd seen through them immediately. She'd known the exact mix of love and discipline that was needed.

She would make a wonderful mother.

He recalled the tension he'd felt in her tonight when he'd told her he wanted kids of his own. She hadn't looked up at him, but her fingers had grown still.

It had hurt him a little, knowing she didn't yet trust him not to crush her hopes and dreams, but he could understand it, too.

He drew the sheet over the twins' shoulders, then silently left the room, wandering next into the studio.

Even after all these years, the faint scent of oil paints and turpentine lingered in the air. He wondered if the odor would disappear once the room held a desk, computer and printer, once the walls were lined with books instead of canvasses.

Do you still love her?

Remembering Shayla's question, Ian shook his head. He wished he could have explained it better. At one time he had loved Joanne with all his heart. But that was long ago. Things were different then. *He* had been different then. While he could remember that he'd once loved Joanne, he couldn't recall the emotion itself.

Now when he thought of love, he thought of Shayla— of her laughter, of the way she talked to herself, of the sweet taste of her mouth and the perfect way she fit against him when he held her in his arms. She filled his thoughts—morning, noon and night. There was no room in his mind or in his heart for another woman, whether real or only a memory.

His gaze moved around the room, over the things that had been Joanne's.

"I won't make the same mistakes again," he pledged to the silence around him. "I won't crush your dreams, Shayla. I won't insist on my own way. Not even about children. Whatever it takes, this marriage is for a lifetime."

He flicked off the lights and headed for his room.

Shayla couldn't sleep. So many things kept racing through her mind, and her heart was torn with conflicting emotions. She hadn't known love was like this, a sweet torment. Joys were greater. Fears were deeper.

She loved Ian with her entire being. She didn't doubt that for an instant. And Ian loved her just as deeply. He seemed to understand her as no one else ever had. And still...

She remembered Ian telling her, weeks ago, not to let anything or anyone get in the way of her dreams. Was she doing that? Once they were married, would her own desire to please him get in the way?

I've always sort of hoped for kids of my own.

She'd known that. Ian had never disguised his desire for a family. But she wasn't ready for babies, for children, for diapers and colic and runny noses, for six-year-olds climbing bookcases and cutting their heads and panicked drives to the emergency room.

Not yet, anyway. She was only thirty. That wasn't old. Women were having babies into their forties these days. There wasn't any rush. Ian seemed willing to wait.

But what if she was *never* ready to give him the family he wanted? Would she be denying the man she loved what would make him happy? Was she merely being selfish? Was her writing worth that?

And if she loved Ian, shouldn't she want to put him first? Maybe she was being unfair to him, accepting his proposal. Maybe she should leave Rainbow Valley, give him a chance to find another woman. The *right* woman for him.

But to leave Ian…she didn't think she could bear that. Just the thought broke her heart.

With a groan, she tossed off the blankets and got out of bed. Her head ached with all her whirling thoughts and questions, but she was unable to shut them off.

She didn't turn on the light. A full moon provided enough illumination for her to see her way out to the living room.

She glanced up at the loft. Anne had come in more than an hour ago; Shayla had feigned sleep when her sister poked her head into the bedroom. She hadn't wanted to talk as the two of them sometimes did in the evening.

Now the loft bedroom was dark and quiet.

Silently Shayla walked to her desk, drawn there like metal to a magnet. She lifted her manuscript out of the stationery box she kept the pages in. What she held in her hands represented many weeks of work. Hard work. Hopefully, good work.

But how did she know? And maybe knowing would provide the answers to all of her other questions. If she was wasting her time…

She drew in a shaky breath. There was only one way to find out if her book was any good. She had to show it to someone. Someone whose opinion mattered. Up to this point, Chet Morrison and True Barry and all the other characters of Eden Valley had belonged only to her. It was time to see what someone else thought of them.

She took another breath—a long, deep one this time— let it out, then laid the manuscript back in its box, her decision made.

It was time to find out if she was truly a writer or merely a dreamer.

Chapter Seventeen

Shayla tried not to let her uncertainties color her joy. This was supposed to be the happiest time of a bride's life, and she was determined it would be so for her.

On Tuesday, she and Anne drove over to the ranch early in the morning to pick up the twins. Then the four of them headed down the highway toward Boise. It didn't take them long to start singing camp songs. Cathy and Angie quickly learned the words to those they hadn't heard before. All mistakes were followed by riotous laughter. More than what they actually deserved.

An hour into their journey, they saw a doe and her fawn along the river's edge. Shayla slowed down so they could all get a better look. The doe, ever alert for danger to her baby, lifted her head and watched the car go by, ready to dart away if necessary. Another fifteen minutes down the road, they stopped to watch a helicopter as it hauled a log out of the forest, the chopper following the river's winding path for a while, then disappearing over a ridge.

As they got closer to Boise, the temperature began to rise. The sun glared down from a cloudless blue sky, and the air conditioner in the compact car couldn't spit out enough cold air to keep the inhabitants comfortable.

It was nearly eleven o'clock before they arrived at their destination. The bridal shop had been recommended by Geneve Barnett, the pastor's wife. Shayla prayed it would be the only stop they would have to make. She hated clothes shopping almost as much as going to the dentist.

"You start looking at bridal gowns," Anne suggested as they walked toward the shop's door, "and the girls and I will check out the bridesmaid and flower girl dresses. That way we can be done in half the time."

"Sounds good to me."

Half an hour later, Shayla was in a fitting room with an overly cheerful saleswoman and a selection of gowns. As soon as the first one—hooped skirt, huge puffy sleeves, and all—was zipped up the back, she knew why she hated shopping so much.

"I thought *all* brides were supposed to be beautiful," she muttered at her reflection. "I look like a cream puff about to explode."

Anne—beautiful, model-like Anne, who looked gorgeous in anything—chose that precise moment to poke her head through the curtains.

"Shayla, I think we found the perfect—" She stopped abruptly and stared a moment in silence before saying, "Oh, it's definitely *not* you, my dear, sweet sister." She entered the fitting room and began to poke through the other gowns. When she was done, she rolled her eyes at

Shayla and said, "You *are* hopeless. None of these are right for you."

"Tell me about it. Maybe I should just get married in shorts and a T-shirt. It's much more my style."

Anne grinned. "I don't think you have to resort to that. I saw something I think would be perfect. Get out of that Scarlett O'Hara thing. I'll be right back."

Without a word, the saleswoman stepped toward Shayla and unzipped the back of the gown, then helped her out of the yards of satin, beads and lace and the voluminous underskirt beneath it all. Anne returned a moment later.

"Don't look until it's on," she instructed. Glancing at the saleswoman, she said, "Would you mind helping the flower girls with their dresses? They're very anxious to try them on. I left them in the next room over."

A look of horror crossed the woman's face, obviously realizing what havoc two unchaperoned six-year-old girls could create in her shop. She hurried out of the fitting room.

"Anne, really," Shayla whispered, fighting a smile.

Her sister chuckled. "Sorry." She didn't sound the least bit repentant. "Turn around and lift your arms over your head. And remember. Don't look until I say so."

"Yes, sir, General, sir."

They laughed together.

But Anne quickly sobered. "Shayla, I've been meaning to say something to you for days, and I can't wait another minute. I want you to know how lucky I am to have you for my big sister. I know I haven't shown it very often, but you've always been there for me, no matter what. Just like letting me come to stay with you for a while. I know I'm in the way—"

"Oh, Anne. That's not true. I never thought—"

"It *is* true. I took advantage of your generous spirit. I knew you wouldn't turn me down. And we're all guilty of it. All us kids and even Mom and Dad. We take advantage of your love for us, and I think we all know it."

Shayla could only shake her head.

"There's something else. I have a confession to make." Anne dropped her gaze. "I read your manuscript while you were gone the other day."

She sucked in a gasp of surprise, then waited anxiously for her sister to continue.

Anne looked up again. "It's wonderful. It truly is. I can't wait to know what happens next. Chet and True are both fabulous characters. And I couldn't figure out who the killer is, even though I'm certain you've introduced him." She nodded. "I'm so proud of you."

Filled with relief, Shayla was afraid she might cry as they exchanged a hug.

A short while later, she lost the battle against tears as she gazed at her reflection. "Oh, Anne." She couldn't believe the bride she saw in the mirror was really her.

Standing behind her, Anne placed her hands on Shayla's shoulders and leaned forward, placing her mouth next to Shayla's ear. "I knew it would be just the thing. You look beautiful, big sister."

And for the first time in her life, Shayla thought maybe she did.

The gown of silk and tulle was understated with simple, flowing lines. It had an old-fashioned look about it that made it perfect for the outdoor ceremony she and Ian had planned.

"I can't believe it's me," she said softly. "Ian won't even recognize me."

"How can you say that? He thinks you're beautiful all the time."

She met her sister's gaze in the mirror. "Do you really think so?"

"Of course I do."

"His first wife was stunning," she said, more to herself than to Anne. "You know. You saw her photograph."

"But he loves *you*, Shayla."

"I know. I know he does. And I love him. More than I thought possible." She turned to face her sister. "What if I'm not the sort of wife he needs? What if I make him terribly unhappy? We're so different, he and I."

Anne shook her head. "Not as different as you think."

"But I'm serious. What if I—"

"I know you're serious. You are also suffering from a raging case of prewedding jitters. That's normal. But get over it. You two are perfect for each other."

"But what if—"

"Miss Vincent?" the saleswoman called from the next room.

"Yes," Shayla and Anne answered in unison. As they looked at each other, they laughed and the tension was broken.

"Could you come here a moment?"

Anne went to see what the saleswoman needed, and Shayla turned back to the mirror.

Please, God, she prayed silently. Let Anne be right. Let me be the right wife for Ian.

"Wait till you see 'em, Uncle Ian," Cathy said excitedly as she tumbled out of Shayla's car.

"They're the prettiest dresses ever!" Angie added, eyes aglow.

Ian ruffled their hair with his hands. "Sounds like you

had a great time." He looked at Shayla who was now standing beside her car.

"We did." She smiled.

There was a glow about her. He hoped he was the cause of it.

To the twins, he said, "You'd better go wash up. Supper's almost ready." Then he moved toward Shayla, eager to hold her in his arms. "I missed you all day long," he whispered before he kissed her.

"I missed you, too," she answered as soon as they came up for air.

"Oh, brother!" That came from Anne as she got out of the car. "Is this mushy behavior going to go on for long?" She sounded disgusted, but there was a definite sparkle of amusement in her eyes.

He winked at Anne, then looked down at Shayla again. "Not for as long as I'd like." He brushed his lips across her forehead. "Not nearly for as long as I'd like."

"Is Ty in the barn?" Anne started walking in that direction even as she spoke. "Maybe I can hitch a ride to the cabin instead of having to suffer you two lovebirds."

"Yeah, he's in there." To Shayla, Ian said, "Will you stay for supper?"

"I should go home. There's a million and one things I've got to do."

"Don't I know it. But another hour won't make that big of a difference. Will it?"

Her arms tightened around his torso. "You're much too tempting for my own good, cowboy."

"I do my dangedest, ma'am."

She laughed softly. "I know you do."

Putting his arm around her shoulders, he walked her toward the house. "I accomplished something today myself. I found a sitter to stay with the girls while I'm working. I decided it wasn't fair of me to ask for your help with the hiring. You have enough to do. Like you just said.''

"Who is it?"

"Nat's sister. Vicky Briscoe. The little blonde that sits next to Hydrangea Zimmerman in the church choir.''

Shayla hesitated, drawing them to a halt just outside the back door to the house. "How old is she?"

"Fifteen, I think. Maybe sixteen.''

"Are you sure she can handle those two? They're a handful sometimes.''

"I'm sure." He gave her a squeeze. "'Course, she'll only be available until school starts, but that'll give us plenty of time to find someone more permanent.'' He grinned. "We can do that after the honeymoon.''

She blushed and lowered her eyes, looking shy, even embarrassed.

In that instant, Ian imagined her on their wedding night, wearing that same innocent expression—and nothing else! Desire raged through him.

Looked like he would need one of those all-too-familiar cold showers before he'd get any sleep tonight.

Shayla knew exactly what Ian was feeling, because she felt it, too.

She often wished they'd eloped as he'd suggested early on. They could have been married three weeks already. She wondered why she'd harbored a single doubt about becoming his wife. All she wanted was to be with him.

"You make my head swim," Ian said, his voice low and husky. "Do you know that?"

She shook her head, then nodded, then shook it again.

"What I wouldn't give for this to be the eighth of August?" He kissed her again, hungrily.

Talk about heads swimming!

"Ian and Shayla sittin' in a tree, *k-i-s-s-i-n-g*."

At the sound of the singsong voices coming from overhead, they broke apart and looked up. The twins were hanging out the window, laughing and pointing.

"What do you think you're doing in that studio?" Ian demanded. "You've been told to stay out of there."

Smiles gone, the two girls instantly disappeared from view.

But he didn't go after them as Shayla had expected him to do. Instead, he embraced her again. "Let 'em sweat for a while," he said with a chuckle.

She raised an eyebrow, then matched his smile before offering her lips for another kiss.

The days that followed were among the happiest of Shayla's life. Full from dawn to dusk, but happy all the same.

There never was a free moment—or so it seemed—to turn on the computer, let alone hours when she was completely alone so she could write. She would have felt guilty, only she hadn't time for that, either.

She talked to her parents several times by phone and made more plans for their arrival in August. She cleaned the house at Paradise and found herself thinking of it as *their* home—Ian's and hers—instead of only *his* home. When she saw that Joanne's photograph was gone from his bedroom, she was touched by his thoughtfulness; she knew then that she would never again wonder if she was merely a replacement for the woman he'd once loved and then lost.

She and Ian went horseback riding some evenings,

just the two of them, while Anne stayed with the children. Blue and Pumpkin carried them high into the mountains, following narrow tracks that normally saw only deer and elk. Most days they ate supper together, and often they sat on the porch swing until after midnight, listening to the sounds of the night, enjoying the feel of holding one another.

Ian's days were full, as well. When Shayla commented on the extralong hours he seemed to be keeping and how tired he looked when he returned from a day on the range, he said he had to do something to work off his frustrations, adding that ranch work was as good a way as any to do it.

His confession made her blush. It also gave her the strangest sense of feminine empowerment. He found her sexy and appealing. Ian desired her. That knowledge continued to surprise and please her.

Not that she wasn't equally frustrated. It seemed she couldn't get enough of being in his arms, surrendering to his sweet-loving attentions. But all the snuggling, hugging and kissing that went on when they were together only made her want him more. And she didn't mean more snuggling, hugging and kissing. She wanted to make love with him. She wanted to know him intimately and forever.

One day, just over two weeks before the wedding, Shayla arrived at the ranch to find the art studio had been emptied of everything except for the bookshelves and the three portraits of Ian. He asked her if she wanted those paintings taken down, too.

"No," she told him, touching the side of his face with her fingertips. "I learned a lot about the man you are from those paintings."

He seemed about to ask her what she meant, but she

stopped him with a slight shake of her head. She wasn't sure she could explain it and didn't want to try.

The next day, a surprise arrived for Cathy and Angie—their own Shetland ponies. Shayla would never forget the looks on their faces when they saw the ponies for the first time. Nor would she forget the expression on Ian's face. Joyful. Excited. Eager.

He was the most wonderful man she'd ever known, she thought as she watched him instructing the twins on how to properly saddle and bridle their ponies. He was so much more than just a good-looking cowboy with a heart-stopping grin. He had a big heart, a big heart full of love that he showered on those around him. Especially on her.

And she loved him so much, it almost hurt. Sometimes the intensity of her feelings for him frightened her. She'd heard it said it was better to have loved and lost than never to have loved at all.

She wondered if that was true.

But then, there was no reason to worry, for she was never going to lose Ian O'Connell. He was going to be her husband, as amazing as that still seemed to her, and she was going to be his wife.

And so the days of July sped into August, rushing toward their wedding day and a bright new future for the two of them.

Shayla knelt on the floor of her bedroom and stared into the box she was packing.

With the rest of the Vincent family arriving from Oregon the next day and only four days remaining until the wedding, she was moving to the ranch house. They'd already taken her office equipment and her clothing over there. This second trip was to pack all the miscellaneous items.

"I don't remember bringing so much with me," she muttered. "Where did it all come from?"

"You're asking *me* a question like that?" Ian laughed as he came to stand behind her. "You already saw how things multiply around my place."

She glanced up. "Your house needs another good cleaning before your mother arrives on Friday. What will she think—"

"Sweetheart…you're fired."

"What?"

"I said you're fired." He took hold of her arm and drew her to her feet. "You are *not* my housekeeper any longer. You're going to be my wife."

"A wife who is *still* needed to clean your house."

"Hey, I—"

She kissed him lightly, stopping his words. When she stepped back, she added, "Get busy, cowboy. I need you to carry out those boxes to the truck."

"Happy to oblige, Miss Vincent." He moved to draw her back into his embrace. "But you're a mighty tempting distraction."

She put a hand flat on his chest, stopping him. "Likewise, Mr. O'Connell, but I'm obviously more self-disciplined than you are." She gave him a tiny shove. "Back to work."

"Shucks." His grin was teasing. "Thought I was a darn sight more irresistible than that."

More than you know, Shayla thought as she determinedly turned away from him.

He kissed the back of her neck, causing shivers to race up and down her spine.

"Ian," she whispered, a gentle rebuke. "My family

arrives tomorrow, and your mother the day after that. We have so much to accomplish and too little time to do it in.''

He released a deep sigh. "Can't blame a guy for trying.''

"Oh, but I *can*. I *do*.'' Despite her words, she was sorely tempted to turn toward him again, to forget herself in the wonderful circle of his arms.

The phone rang.

"Ignore it,'' he said softly, then nibbled her earlobe.

She sucked in some air. Her eyes closed. Gooseflesh rose on her arms.

"Ever tell you how good you smell?'' He nuzzled the opposite side of her neck.

The phone continued to ring.

She opened her eyes. The bed was only a few short steps in front of her. Anne had taken the twins to McCall. They had no one to interrupt them. They could just—

She groaned as she hurried out of the bedroom to answer the telephone.

"Hello?''

"Hello. May I speak to Shayla Vincent, please?''

"This is she.''

"Ms. Vincent, this is Bradley Karnes of Masterson Publishing House in New York.''

Her heart stopped. "Yes?'' There was a strange buzzing in her ears.

"I'm an acquiring editor for Masterson. I've read your submission, Ms. Vincent, and…''

From the doorway of the bedroom, Ian watched and listened, a sense of doom perched on his shoulder.

"Three weeks?''

He couldn't be certain from her expression or the tone of her voice what she was feeling. It didn't seem to be bad news on the other end of the line, and yet...

"Well, I suppose..." Her brows drew together in a frown. "But you see, in a few days, I'll be getting..." A lengthy silence as she listened, then, "Yes, I understand."

She glanced toward the bedroom, saw Ian standing there, turned away.

His sense of doom darkened, grew heavier. He took a step forward.

"By the end of August. Yes, I believe I can do that. I'll do my best. Thank you, Mr. Karnes." She reached for a pad of paper and a pencil and began scribbling notes on it. "Yes, I will... No, I don't think so... Of course... Yes, and thank you again, Mr. Karnes. Goodbye."

Ian took another couple of steps toward the kitchen.

"They're interested in my book," Shayla said softly. Then she turned toward him. Her eyes were wide with surprise. "They might want to buy it."

Chapter Eighteen

"Buy your book?" Ian strode toward her, trying to ignore his growing apprehension. "But honey, that's wonderful." He embraced her, squeezing tightly.

"I sent him the first three chapters," Shayla said, her voice muffled against his chest. "The editor wants the completed book by the end of August."

Ian drew back slightly. "And?" he prompted as he stared down into her eyes.

"And I don't have it finished. I need at least another hundred and fifty pages. Maybe more."

His mouth was dry. His heart was pounding.

"There's no way I can get it finished between now and the end of August. Not with the wedding and the honeymoon and everything else."

"Then we'll postpone the honeymoon."

"You would do that for me?"

"No," he replied softly. "I would do it for us."

Tears sprang into her eyes. "He didn't guarantee they would buy it. We might be putting off the honeymoon for no reason."

"But it wouldn't be for no reason. This is the chance you've been hoping for."

"Thank you." She placed the palm of her right hand against his left cheek. "Thank you for understanding."

Truth was, he wasn't nearly as understanding as she believed him to be. In his heart, he was torn in two. He honestly wanted to help her achieve her goal of being published, but there was a part of him that felt a twinge of anger, too.

Why now? Why did this have to happen now?

Shayla stepped out of his arms. "It will mean long hours closed away in my office. I'm not a fast writer, and my outline is still a bit sketchy." She turned away. "Maybe I should have told Mr. Karnes there was no way I could do it."

"You'll do it, sweetheart." He laid his hands on her shoulders. "I have faith in you."

He felt a tiny shudder pass through her.

"Let's get to work," he said, turning her toward him again. "We've got to finish packing and get you over to the ranch. You have words to write."

"But I—"

"No buts." He gave her a smile he didn't feel. "This'll all work out. You'll see."

Shayla closed her eyes as she leaned back in her office chair. "Done," she whispered.

Despite the time it had taken to get her office equipment up and running, she had managed to write ten pages today. It was a momentum she hoped she could continue. It wasn't going to be easy. Especially once her family arrived.

She glanced at the clock. Almost midnight.

She smiled tenderly, remembering the way Ian had tapped on her door when it was time for the twins to go to bed. He hadn't wanted to disturb her, but he hadn't wanted to disappoint Cathy and Angie, either. The girls had both wanted to say good-night to their "almost aunt."

She was so blessed, she thought as she closed out of her word processing program and shut down her computer. She still couldn't believe how willing Ian had been to postpone their honeymoon, just to give her a chance at selling her novel. How many men would have done that? Not many.

Yes, she was blessed indeed.

Still smiling to herself, she turned out the light and made her way to the bedroom closest to the staircase. This was her room until after the wedding; then she would move into the master bedroom.

Her stomach fluttered as she glanced over her shoulder, gazing down the hallway. Ian was in that bedroom now, sleeping. In just four more days, she would be sharing that bed with him, falling to sleep with his arms around her. She could scarcely believe it, even now.

She wondered if True would ever know this much happiness with Chet.

After putting on a nightshirt and following her normal bedtime routine of washing her face and brushing her teeth, Shayla crawled beneath the sheet and blanket, then turned off the bedside lamp, plunging the room into darkness.

Surprisingly, considering all there was to think

about—Ian, her novel, her family, the wedding—she fell asleep almost the moment her head hit the pillow.

It was the calm before the storm.

The Vincent family arrived in their rented van at eleven o'clock the next morning. Ian was at the ranch house to greet them, along with Shayla, Anne and the twins.

Ian was aware of several things as Shayla introduced him to her parents, Reba and Doug; her brothers, Dwight, Ken and George; and her younger two sisters, Olivia and Crystal. First, that they were a noisy bunch; there was lots of talking and laughing. Second, that they were a genuinely loving family; the kissing and hugging was done in earnest and not out of obligation. And third, that their presence had an immediate—and not necessarily positive—effect on Shayla.

It took him a while to figure out what it was. That she loved them all was obvious. Her delight in catching up on what had been happening to each of them since she left Oregon was real. So what was it that bothered him?

Shayla invited everyone inside for a tour of the house. Her mother was as impressed by the large kitchen as Shayla had said she would be. Her father asked Ian lots of questions about the age of the house and how it had been built and about how the O'Connells had come to the valley early in the century.

The tour moved outside. Crystal, at thirteen, was delighted by the dogs, especially Honey Girl, and immediately asked her parents if she couldn't have a pup from the next litter. Olivia took more notice of the two ranch hands who were doctoring an injured heifer in the barn; Anne made certain her younger sister understood that Ty was off-limits. The three brothers seemed most interested in the news that Shayla had taken up horseback riding, all of them expressing more than a little surprise and disbelief.

Ian put a possessive arm around Shayla's back and gave her a squeeze. "I think you'd be surprised by a lot of the things your sister can do." He would have continued, might have blurted out the news about her book, but she stopped him with a slight shake of her head.

They all returned to the house where Shayla served a lunch of grilled hamburgers and tossed salad in the dining room.

Ian learned more about the Vincent family over the course of that meal, and toward the end, he finally realized what it was about Shayla that was different. She had suddenly become the caretaker of them all, while at the same time becoming almost invisible to everyone in the room.

Ian couldn't claim to be an expert in pop psychology. But even a cowboy from Idaho could see what was happening before his eyes. And he didn't like it much. He remembered the animated young woman he'd first seen on the deck of her cabin. That wasn't who he saw before him now.

His gaze met with Anne's, and her eyes seemed to say to him, *See what I mean?*

Yeah, he saw.

Shayla stared at the computer monitor, watching the cursor blink on an otherwise totally blank screen. It was nearly five in the morning. She'd been at her desk all night, and she'd written nothing. Absolutely nothing.

Of course, she hadn't been able to get to her new office until nearly midnight. Even after taking her family over to the cabin and getting them settled in, it hadn't quieted down. There'd been several phone calls from her siblings, asking where this or that was. Then Cathy and Angie had gotten into an argument about whose turn it was to feed the dogs for Uncle Ian. He wasn't present, of course. He'd had to drive over to the cabin with extra blankets. The twins' argument had turned to spiteful, hurtful words, followed by buckets of tears. It had taken Shayla nearly fifteen minutes to comfort both girls and get them settled in for the night.

Elbows on the desk, she rested her forehead against the heels of her hands. "I'm so tired, I can't think." She wanted to weep.

She straightened, rose from her chair and walked to the window. The horizon was beginning to show the first traces of dawn. She could make out the shadowy forms of horses grazing in the paddock. All was silent. Not even a breeze stirred the trees. It was a beautiful scene, so seductively tranquil. But that was deceiving.

It wouldn't be tranquil later today or the day after that.

Or the week after that.

Or the month after that.

Ian's mother would arrive this afternoon. All of the Vincents would be in and out of the ranch house until after the wedding. The twins would be here until at least next spring. And Ian wanted children of his own.

She loved him. She loved him desperately, with everything she was. But it wasn't going to work. She would get hurt in the end and so would he. She wouldn't be what he wanted. She *couldn't* be. Better to end it now. Better for them both.

She heard the door open behind her and knew it was Ian.

"I can't marry you," she said over the lump in her throat and the ache in her chest.

She heard the door close and turned around.

Ian's expression was grim as he stared at her.

"I can't marry you," she repeated.

"Why not?"

"I just can't."

He didn't cross the room, didn't try to change her mind by taking her into his arms. He simply watched her.

"It costs too much." She dropped her gaze to the floor. "I'll never be a writer if I stay. I'll give in. I'll give up."

He remained silent.

For some reason that made her angry. "I want to be a writer. I need to finish this book, and I can't the way things are. It was *you* who told me not to let anything get in the way of my dreams." She cast a challenging glance in his direction.

"I remember." His voice was flat, emotionless.

"Then you should understand."

"I understand better than you think I do." He released a sigh as he raked his fingers through his hair, then softly added, "I understand all too well."

"I'm sorry. I should have realized before now that I couldn't go through with it. I should have—"

"Want to know what I think?" he interrupted, louder this time, a hint of anger in his voice. "I think you're using your writing as an excuse to run away. You're afraid, and it isn't because of the book."

"I haven't been able to write a single page all night long."

"That's just an excuse. You're afraid to depend on anyone else. You take care of everybody because then you'll be too dang busy to open up your heart and let them in. Really inside. You're afraid of the cost of loving, not the cost of losing a dream.'' He patted his chest with his hand. ''I wanted you to let *me* in. I wanted you to lean on *me*. You *could* have trusted me, Shayla, if you'd only trusted yourself first.''

He put his hand on the doorknob and turned it. But then he stopped and looked at her again.

''I made the mistake once before of standing in the way of someone's dream. I wasn't going to make that mistake again, Shayla. I wouldn't have made that mistake with you. I already told you that. I already tried to prove that to you.'' He opened the door. ''So you go if you have to. Just remember that I love you, and I'll be right here if you change your mind.''

It was just before seven o'clock when Shayla drove away from the house at Paradise Ranch. Her hastily packed suitcase was in the trunk, along with her computer and printer and manuscript. In the rearview mirror, she saw Ian, sitting astride Blue, watching as she left him. He had let her go without a word. He'd simply let her go.

She was about ten miles down the highway before she realized she was crying so hard she couldn't see the road. She blinked and wiped her eyes, then looked for a place to turn off, knowing she wouldn't be able to stop the tears for long. Around the next bend in the road, she found a small campground alongside the river.

She was glad it was deserted. She didn't want strangers watching her crumble.

I wanted you to let me in. I wanted you to lean on me.

She rested her forehead on the back of her hands, hands that still gripped the steering wheel.

You could have trusted me, Shayla, if you'd only trusted yourself first.

Memories drifted through her mind. Ian working with a young foal. Ian roping cattle. Ian fixing sandwiches in the kitchen. Ian playing with the twins and roughhousing with the dogs. Ian teaching her to ride, showing so much patience. Ian holding her in his arms, kissing her, loving her.

He was right. He hadn't tried to take away her dream. He'd wanted to share in it.

It wasn't losing her dreams she was afraid of. It was trusting someone with her heart.

She got out of the car and walked to the river's edge, watching as it churned and foamed, roaring over the submerged boulders and logs that lined the riverbed.

That's how she felt. As if her insides were churning and foaming and roaring.

She sat on the ground, pulled up her knees toward her chest. With her arms clasped around her shins, she pressed her face against her knees and allowed herself to cry.

With his heart pounding in fear, Ian sped down the highway. He shouldn't have let her go. He never should have told her he wouldn't stand in her way. Ten years ago he'd let another woman drive out of his life—and she'd died that day.

This time he had to do it right. If he were to lose Shayla…

Rounding a turn in the road, he saw the roof of her car, parked in a campground. He breathed a silent prayer of thanksgiving as he braked and pulled off the road. He got out of his truck, not bothering to close the door behind him. Her car was empty, but his gaze soon found her, sitting beside the river. He stopped about ten feet away, realizing that she hadn't heard his arrival above the thunder of the river.

She was crying. Her shoulders were shaking.

Was he making a mistake? Should he let her go? Maybe she was right. Maybe he would be in her way. Maybe…

She lifted her head and turned toward him as if she'd suddenly sensed his presence. Her eyes glittered with tears.

No, he wasn't making a mistake.

He crossed the ground that separated them, took hold of her arms and drew her to her feet. "Don't go. Don't leave me."

"Oh, Ian."

He drew her closer to him. "Without you, Paradise Ranch won't mean anything to me. It'll be too empty without you in it. I need you, Shayla, and I think you need me, too. Don't give up on us without a fight."

"You were right about me. I'm afraid. It's easier to run away *before* I get hurt."

"Then stop running." He brushed the hair back from her forehead. "You don't have to be afraid. I love you. I believe in you. I won't hurt you."

She gave her head a tiny shake. "I blamed everyone else for what was wrong with my life. For my dismal little apartment and my boring job. For having to put off my dreams. For not writing my stories. Even for not finding a man and falling in love. But it was really only me standing in my own way." She released a sad little laugh. "Wasn't it?"

He kissed her with all the tenderness his heart possessed, hoping beyond hope that she would understand how much she was cherished, how important she was in his life. He would move heaven and earth to make her happy—if she would give him the chance.

When their lips parted, Shayla looked up into his eyes for the longest time. So long, he thought he couldn't bear it. And then she smiled.

"Take me to Paradise, cowboy. Take me home."

Epilogue

While the deputies placed handcuffs on Mitchell Jones in the glow of the spinning red lights atop the police car, Chet pulled True into his arms.

"So help me, woman, if you ever cause me this much trouble again..."

He didn't finish the threat. He didn't have to.

"Cowboy..." She smiled that sexy, unapologetic smile that was True's alone. "I plan to cause you nothing but trouble from here on out, and you know it."

Yeah, he knew it. And he didn't care. He wanted whatever kind of trouble she dished out. In fact, he would welcome it.

He kissed her. Hard. Branding her with his mouth. He wanted everybody to see him kissing her. He wanted the word to spread across Eden Valley like a grass fire: True Barry belonged to Chet Morrison.

And the next guy to forget it was going to wish he was sitting in a prison cell next to Mitchell Jones.

True must have understood what Chet was thinking, for when their lips parted, she gave him another one of her sultry smiles, the kind that made his blood run hot and his brain turn to mush.

To think he'd once thought himself immune to her. What a joke!

"Come on, cowboy," she whispered huskily. "I'm in the mood for some of that trouble right now."

"I reckon I'll be happy to oblige, ma'am. Right happy to oblige."

Shayla lifted the last sheet of paper out of the printer tray and stared at it.

"The end," she whispered, then grinned. "I made it."

She wanted to shout, but it was two in the morning and she didn't want to wake the twins.

"Time to celebrate?"

At the sound of Ian's voice, Shayla swiveled her chair around. Her husband stood in the doorway, wearing a pair of Levi's, his chest and feet bare, a bottle of champagne and two glasses in his hands.

"How did you know?" she asked.

He shrugged. "I just had a feeling you would wrap it up tonight." He smiled at her. "So how did it turn out?"

"Mystery solved. Bad guy in jail. Chet gets the girl."

"Lucky Chet."

She returned his smile before saying, "There's still a lot of editing to do before I can ship it to New York, and only three days to do it in."

"I've got faith in you, sweetheart. You'll get it done in time."

He closed the door to her office with his heel and

crossed the room to her desk. He set the champagne bottle and glasses down, then drew Shayla up from her chair.

"I'd like to kiss the author of *Trouble in Eden*, if that's all right with her. After all, I've never kissed a mystery novelist before."

She snuggled close, enjoying the feel of his work-hardened body, loving how familiar it was to her after twenty days of wedded bliss.

Staring up into his beloved face, she allowed herself a few moments to indulge in remembering all that had happened during those past twenty days.

The wedding ceremony had been more beautiful than anything she could have anticipated. Almost the entire population of Rainbow Valley had turned out to witness the marriage of a favorite son to the flatlander from Portland, Oregon. Even the heavens had seemed joyous, for there hadn't been a single cloud in the bright blue sky, and a soft breeze had kept the day from being too warm.

With the twins looking on with mischievous grins of approval, Ian and Shayla had exchanged their vows, each of them pledging their love in words they'd composed themselves. Although she couldn't recall Ian's vows word for word, she had only to remember the way he'd looked as he'd spoken them to bring tears to her eyes again.

Shayla's family had surprised the newlyweds by turning her cabin into a honeymoon suite, complete with an elegant wedding supper, champagne, bouquets of roses and wildflowers. Then, leaving the bride and groom alone for their one-night honeymoon, the Vincent clan had bedded down at the ranch, guests of Ian's mother and the twins. They'd left for Portland first thing in the morning. Much to Ty's disappointment, Anne had gone with the rest of the family.

Of course Shayla hadn't noticed their absence. She'd been too diverted by the attentions of her husband. She'd anticipated his lovemaking for weeks before she'd become his bride, and he'd more than fulfilled her fantasies on their wedding night and in the nights that followed.

Now she anticipated his lovemaking even more than before. Now she knew what Ian could do with one tender touch, one gentle stroke. Now she knew what it meant to lie with him in the center of their king-size bed; to feel her heart racing in time with his, beat for beat; to be joined with him in an ancient dance of passion, an act as old as time itself and yet so uniquely their own.

With those images filling her thoughts, she whispered, "Go ahead. Kiss the mystery novelist, Mr. O'Connell. She's waiting."

The kiss that followed was similar to the one she'd written about only minutes before. It was like being branded. A thrill of desire coiled through her.

"Want to know what else I've never done?" he whispered when their lips parted.

She looked up at him, starry-eyed.

"I've never made love to a mystery novelist."

Her blood ran a few degrees hotter. Her body tingled in anticipation.

"I think we should explore this new relationship." He swept her feet off the floor and headed for the door.

"What about the champagne?" she asked, not really caring.

"Don't need it. I'm already intoxicated...." His laugh was low, husky and full of secret meanings. "By you."

She pressed her cheek against his chest and closed her eyes, reveling in the wonders of everything he made her feel. Loved. Cherished. Beautiful. Special. So many things she'd never expected.

And it was all because of Ian.

He'd made even those things she'd never dared to dream come true.

He set her down at the foot of their bed. Tenderly he brushed her unruly hair away from her face. Then he rained light kisses everywhere. On her forehead. On the tip of her nose. On her eyelids. On her cheek and throat and earlobes. And all the while his fingers nimbly disrobed her.

When she thought she could bear the waiting no more, he stopped, holding perfectly still.

She opened her eyes, meeting his gaze.

"I love you, Shayla O'Connell," he said softly, gravely. "I always will."

"I know." She smiled—imagining it just might be a True Barry smile—and whispered, "Take me to paradise, cowboy."

"Happy to oblige, ma'am."

And then her cowboy took her there, just as he'd promised.

* * * * *

Silhouette SPECIAL EDITION

presents **THE BRIDAL CIRCLE**, a brand-new miniseries honoring friendship, family and love...

THE BRIDAL CIRCLE

by

Andrea Edwards

They dreamed of marrying and leaving their small town behind—but soon discovered there's no place like home for true love!

IF I ONLY HAD A...HUSBAND (May '99)
Penny Donnelly had tried desperately to forget charming millionaire Brad Corrigan. But her heart had a memory—and a will—of its own. And Penny's heart was set on Brad becoming her husband....

SECRET AGENT GROOM (August '99)
When shy-but-sexy Heather Mahoney bumbles onto secret agent Alex Waterstone's undercover mission, the only way to protect the innocent beauty is to claim her as his lady love. Will Heather carry out her own secret agenda and claim Alex as her groom?

PREGNANT & PRACTICALLY MARRIED (November '99)
Pregnant Karin Spencer had suddenly lost her memory and *gained* a pretend fiancé. Though their match was make-believe, Jed McCarron was her dream man. Could this bronco-bustin' cowboy give up his rodeo days for family ways?

Available at your favorite retail outlet.

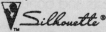

The combination of physical attraction and danger can be explosive!

Coming in July 1999
three steamy romances together in one book

HOT PURSUIT

by bestselling authors

JOAN JOHNSTON

ANNE STUART

MALLORY RUSH

Joan Johnston—A WOLF IN SHEEP'S CLOTHING
The Hazards and the Alistairs had been feuding for generations, so when Harriet Alistair laid claim to her great-uncle's ranch, Nathan Hazard was at his ornery worst. But then he saw her and figured it was time to turn on the charm, forgive, forget…and seduce?

Anne Stuart—THE SOLDIER & THE BABY
What could possibly bring together a hard-living, bare-chested soldier and a devout novice? At first, it was an innocent baby…and then it was a passion hotter than the simmering jungle they had to escape from.

Mallory Rush—LOVE SLAVE
Rand Slick hired Rachel Tinsdale to infiltrate the dark business of white slavery. It was a risky assignment, Rachel knew. But even more dangerous was her aching desire for her sexy, shadowy client.…

Available at your favorite retail outlet.

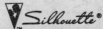

Silhouette SPECIAL EDITION®

LINDSAY McKENNA

delivers two more exciting books in her heart-stopping new series:

MORGAN'S MERCENARIES
II
THE HUNTERS

Coming in July 1999:
HUNTER'S WOMAN
Special Edition #1255

Ty Hunter wanted his woman back from the moment he set his piercing gaze on her. For despite the protest on Dr. Catt Alborak's soft lips, Ty was on a mission to give the stubborn beauty everything he'd foolishly denied her once—his heart, his soul—and most of all, his child....

And coming in October 1999:
HUNTER'S PRIDE
Special Edition #1274

Devlin Hunter had a way with the ladies, but when it came to his job as a mercenary, the brooding bachelor worked alone. Until his latest assignment paired him up with Kulani Dawson, a feisty beauty whose tender vulnerabilities brought out his every protective instinct—and chipped away at his proud vow to never fall in love....

Look for the exciting series finale in early 2000—when MORGAN'S MERCENARIES: THE HUNTERS comes to Silhouette Desire®!

Available at your favorite retail outlet.

Silhouette®

Look us up on-line at: http://www.romance.net   SSEMM

Silhouette®SPECIAL EDITION®
AND SILHOUETTE® Desire®
The Bachelor Bet

*In bestselling author **Joan Elliott Pickart's** engaging new series, three bachelor friends have bet that marriage and family will never be a part of their lives. But they'll learn never to bet against love....*

TAMING TALL, DARK BRANDON
Desire #1223, June 1999

Brandon Hamilton had long ago given up on the idea of home, hearth and babies. But when he meets stubborn beauty Andrea Cunningham, he finds himself in danger of being thoroughly and irrevocably tamed....

THE IRRESISTIBLE MR. SINCLAIR
Special Edition #1256, July 1999

Taylor Sinclair believes marriage is for fools, but he reconsiders when he falls for Janice Jennings—a secretly stunning woman who hides behind a frumpy disguise. A barrier Taylor vows to breach...

THE MOST ELIGIBLE M.D.
Special Edition #1262, August 1999

She's a woman without a past. He's a man without a future. Still, **Dr. Ben Rizzoli** cannot quell his passion for the delicate amnesiac who's made him live and love—and long for the family he believes he can never have....

*Don't miss **Joan Elliott Pickart's** newest series, **The Bachelor Bet**— in Silhouette Desire and Silhouette Special Edition!*
Available at your favorite retail outlet.

▼ Silhouette®

SDTBB

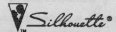

*This August 1999, the legend
continues in Jacobsville*

DIANA PALMER

LOVE WITH A
LONG, TALL TEXAN

A trio of brand-new short stories featuring
three irresistible Long, Tall Texans

GUY FENTON, LUKE CRAIG
and CHRISTOPHER DEVERELL...

This August 1999, Silhouette brings readers an
extra-special collection for Diana Palmer's legions
of fans. Diana spins three unforgettable stories of
love—Texas-style! Featuring the men you can't get
enough of from the wonderful town of Jacobsville,
this collection is a treasure for all fans!

*They grow 'em tall in the saddle in Jacobsville—and
they're the best-looking, sweetest-talking men to be
found in the entire Lone Star state. They are proud,
hardworking men of steel and it will take
the perfect woman to melt their hearts!*

**Don't miss this collection of original
Long, Tall Texans stories...available in
August 1999 at your favorite retail outlet.**